MORE
AFRICAN
ADVENTURES

Stubby Stories No. 3

By

Lloyd Fezler

Cover by: Colonnade Graphics, El Cajon, CA
Illustrated by: Sheila Hinderer, El Cajon, CA

MASTER BOOK PUBLISHERS
EL CAJON, CALIFORNIA
92020

More African Adventures
(Stubby Stories No. 3)

Copyright © 1984

MASTER BOOK PUBLISHERS, A Division of CLP
111 S. Marshall Avenue
El Cajon, California 92020

Library of Congress Catalog Card Number 84-62232
ISBN 0-89051-105-5

Cataloging in Publication Data

Fezler, Lloyd 1918-
  More African Adventures.

  (Stubby Stories Adventures, No. 3)
  Title.
                          813
ISBN 0-89051-105-5

Printed in the United States of America

About the Author

Dr. Lloyd LeRoy Fezler was born in Osakis, Minnesota. He spent his childhood, youth, and adolescence in that small rural town. His memories of that community, nestled on the shore of a beautiful lake, are impregnated with fondness.

The late high school years of his life were filled with dreams that encompassed being a "big league" baseball player, but these dreams were never fulfilled. Days prior to graduation from high school, a severe injury brought him to death's door. His dreams were shattered by the effects.

After a two-year recovery period, his family encouraged him to pursue a teaching career. Four years later he received a Bachelor of Science degree, with majors in science and social studies. The teaching of science (biology, chemistry, and physics) became his speciality.

While his children were young, the Stubby Stories came into existence. They were originated while Dr. Fezler was away attending summer school. The first twenty-one stories ("Adventures at Mountain Haven") were designed for his two youngest children.

As time passed, Dr. Fezler was selected to go to Africa

as a member of the Teacher Education Program in East Africa. For three years he was stationed in Kenya. There he became acquainted with the life patterns of several species of wild animals. Thousands of pictures were taken.

Two years after returning to the United States, he was selected to go to Thailand. It was while living in Bangkok that the "African Adventures" were written for three young ladies who became his godchildren. It is to these children, godchildren, and "son" Walter that the stories are primarily dedicated, with a feeling of deep appreciation for the beauty given to life.

The author extends a special thanks to Mr. Meeker and his family for their encouragement, to Dr. Henry Morris for introducing the stories to the publisher, and to JoJo for her inspiration.

It is Dr. Fezler's greatest desire that "tiny" Stubby will help someone find a "big" love for Lord Jesus.

Chapter One

Another day was beginning. Today, the little men, Abdi, and Doc were going to take another look within the Reserve for Patience and her cubs. The end of the African safari was not many days away. The tiny men and Doc would be heading home.

Before leaving, they all hoped to find the spotted cats with the tear-streaked faces once more.

Stubby and Bobby wondered just how big the cubs would be. It had been several weeks since the cheetah family disappeared, and Doc had told them cheetahs grow fast, so the two little men didn't know what to expect. Maybe they wouldn't even recognize the cubs.

For a good reason, Stubby was sure the spotted lady and her cubs would be found. He knew God would help even with things that many people might believe are not important. The little man smiled. He whispered, "Thank you, God for your special help with one little thing — and I do mean Bobby."

The sun had climbed high in the sky and no cheetahs had been seen, but while searching along the ridges, a herd of zebras was found.

Abdi drove into the valley for a closer look at the herd, but he did not go very near them as he did not want to frighten the animals with the striped suits.

Doc said, "You will notice that very young zebras have brown stripes. Brown is harder to see when the zebra lies in grass. As the young colt or filly gets older

One giraffe had
its front legs
spread out
wide.

its stripes become black. In the bushes, black is harder to see. I used to believe it was all accidental, but after years of study I know it is God's plan.

The four men did not stay with the zebra herd more than a few minutes. Then Abdi drove to a salt lick.

A salt lick is a place where there is salt for the animals to lick up from the ground if they want to. In some places, Abdi's rangers throw the salt on the soil, but there are places where the ground is salty all the time.

On the salt lick, there were giraffes, zebras, and a pair of ostriches. One giraffe had its front legs spread out wide. A twiga, the Swahili word meaning giraffe, must spread its front legs if it wants to get its mouth down to the ground.

If a twiga stands with its head down and its feet spread, it is very tipsy. A push behind and the giraffe could end up with its back feet off the ground, while it stood on its front legs and nose.

When the little men saw how hard it was for a giraffe to get its mouth down to the ground, it was easy to understand why twigas do not eat grass as much as they eat leaves from bushes and trees.

Bobby shouted excitedly. "Look," he said, "over there! It's a little giraffe. Is it a midget twiga or a baby?"

Abdi drove in a circle around the baby twiga. The giraffe looked much like a wooly, stuffed toy. It turned its head and stared at the men in the Rover.

"It must be only a few minutes old." Stubby said, "It is still wet from being born. See how damp it is on the side not touched by the sun. If it was just born, how come it is standing up?"

"My people," Abdi said, "say that sometimes twiga babies are born while their mother is standing up, so the baby giraffe is born standing up. But I am not sure because I have not seen it happen. Perhaps their stories are true."

The African and Doc told the two little tourists that twiga babies are usually about five feet tall when they are born.

Doc said, "Baby twigas should be tall. A mother giraffe is about fourteen feet tall. This kind of giraffe is the Masai variety. Other kinds may be even taller."

Shortly after circling the baby twiga, the Land Rover was driven through some scattered gumwood trees. A flock of vultures was on the ground eating the left-overs from a big cat kill. When Abdi and Doc saw that the head end had not been eaten, they were sure the kill had been made by a cheetah. It was a mid-morning kill, so they thought a cheetah must be close by.

The African drove in a big circle around the kill as four pairs of eyes searched for cheetahs.

Not far away, two big male cheetahs lay in the shade under a tree. When Abdi drove quite close, they did not move. Abdi kept the motor running.

The spotted cats had their ears turned toward the Rover, but their eyes were busy watching a mother black rhino. The mother rhino was walking along a grass covered hillside. Tripping along behind the lady rhinoceros was a young rhino.

Stubby said, "I think those male cheetahs are trying to hide. Are they afraid of the rhino? Of course, a rhinoceros is much bigger and stronger than a spotted cat, but a cheetah can easily run away."

If the rhinos kept following the path on which they were walking, they would go very close to the cheetahs.

"A rhinoceros," Doc said, "is believed to have poor eyes, but a very good nose and two good ears. They are surprisingly fast runners and very strong."

Abdi asked, "What is the direction of the wind? If she smells those cats, she will charge."

At first, the rhino was walking along the side of the Rover, but the path curved and crossed behind it.

The mother rhino was walking along a grass covered hillside. Tripping along behind the lady rhinoceros was a young rhino.

Suddenly the mother rhino stopped. She turned and looked at the Land Rover.

Abdi said, "I'm sure she smells the cheetahs. Can you see how her nose is testing the breeze?"

The rhino stood very still for only a moment, then she began to trot faster and faster toward the Land Rover.

Almost together, Stubby and Doc shouted, "She is coming after us. Let's get out of here!"

The African stepped hard on the gas pedal. The Rover kicked up a cloud of dust as its wheels dug into the dirt.

Abdi shouted, "Come on Rover, let's get going — and fast!"

Doc yelled, "Stubby, you and Bobby get down on the floor. Mother rhino is gaining on us. She will catch us for sure unless we have a miracle."

The lady black rhino was very close to the back end of the Rover.

Stubby prayed, "God, we need You again. Please help us!"

When the rhino began her charge, the male cheetahs stood up. As she bolted toward the Rover and the cheetahs, one of the spotted cats ran through the narrow gap between the Rover and the angry rhino.

When the mother rhino saw the male cheetah, she slid to a halt. A moment later, she chased after the spotted cat.

Even with a full stomach, the male cat easily outran the angry rhino. The big cat with the tear-streaked face ran in a circle. Soon he was so far away and the wind was just right so the black rhino could not see, hear, or smell him.

After completing a circle the male cheetah once again rested in the shade with his friend.

Abdi said, "Maybe you should thank your God."

Stubby answered, "Abdi, why don't you thank Him? He is your God too."

The rhinos moved out of sight and Abdi went back to where the cheetahs rested. When he let the Rover chug slowly up close to the spotted cats, one of them snarled. The big cat looked dangerous.

The African said, "It is only an act. It is true a cheetah will try to scare us, but I have never heard of a wild cheetah hurting a person. I am going to open the door. Just watch what happens."

Warden Abdi opened the door, and both male cheetahs kicked up dust as they ran away. All four men laughed and laughed.

The radio in the Land Rover crackled. A voice said, "Calling Warden Abdi. Calling Warden Abdi. Come in please. This is Ranger Kerich."

Abdi answered, then the ranger spoke rapidly in Swahili.

Warden Abdi's eyes sparkled when he signed off. He said, "Hang on very tight. I am going to drive fast. Sorry, but we must hurry."

The Rover raced across the grasslands and bounced over small rocks and holes. Stubby and Bobby almost fell to the floor more than once.

Bobby whispered, "I feel as if I am riding a wild horse and it sure is bucking hard. Why are we hurrying so fast?"

Stubby said, "I don't know, but it must be something important or exciting."

Finally, Abdi slowed the Rover. When he was still at least fifty meters from a herd of impalas, he stopped.

On a hillside, the herd of red antelopes was grazing. As the impalas grazed, they moved closer and closer to a small clump of bushes. Although the grass on the hillside was dry, dust covered, and brown, the leaves on the bushes were quite green. Bobby wondered if the impalas would eat the green leaves.

Warden Abdi pointed his finger at a big green bush.

He said, "There is something under that bush. If the impalas are not careful, it could be very exciting. Keep your eyes on that bush."

Bobby and Stubby looked and looked. They could not see anything under the bush.

Stubby said, "Well, whatever it is I'd bet it isn't a lion, leopard, or a cheetah."

"It must have gone away. I sure can't see anything big enough to hurt an impala," Bobby said.

What was in that big bush? Was it in the bush or under the bush? Why didn't Abdi drive closer? It was not easy to see something fifty meters away.

Abdi looked at Bobby as he squirmed and squirmed while trying to see under the bush.

The black African smiled at Bobby. "You must learn," he said, "to be patient. Waiting is not easy for a young man, but as your people say 'Patience is a virtue'."

Chapter Two

The two little men, along with Warden Abdi and Doc, sat quietly in the Rover, watching a herd of impalas. The red antelopes grazed on a nearby hillside. The hillside was bare of trees, but it did have one clump of bushes. The bushes were about 75 meters from the impala heard. The Rover was parked to one side of the bushes. Abdi had said there was something under those bushes, but Bobby had looked and looked without seeing anything. Bobby thought, "Whatever was there must be gone."

As he sat watching the red antelopes, Bobby counted them. There were nineteen females, several young kids, and one male impala. The big male, or buck, antelope was the herd leader.

When Doc saw the leader, he said, "Look at that big buck impala. Isn't he a beauty? Those long curved horns have helped him win many fights, I would be willing to bet. To be a herd leader that buck has had to drive all other males away from the herd."

Bobby said, "He sure acts like a champion. That herd leader seems to be very proud. How big do impalas get?"

Abdi explained, "Bucks or males may get to be as heavy as 180-190 pounds, but more commonly they weight around 150 pounds. Females are smaller. Usually they weigh from 100-130 pounds. Have you noticed that lady impalas do not have any horns?"

In a loud whisper, Doc said, "You better keep your eyes open. I think there is trouble ahead for that lady impala. I mean the red antelope who is not staying with the herd."

A female impala had strayed from the herd and was moving toward a clump of bushes. She was out in front of the other herd members.

Little Bobby said, "I'll bet the green leaves on those bushes really look good to the lady antelope. I hope she likes them."

The male impala was standing outlined against the Ngong Hills. He was looking across the grasslands.

The herd leader turned around. He saw the lady impala as she hurried toward the bushes. The leader snorted in anger and trotted after her. He did not want any of his ladies to leave the herd, but this lady was already several meters in front of the others.

Once again, the big buck snorted to show his anger and now he loped after the female to get her back to the herd.

The female impala reached the bushes and lifted her head to nibble the green leaves, but she never had a chance to taste them.

Suddenly, something that looked like a big branch from a tree shot out from under the bushes. In a flash, it grabbed the lady impala and wrapped itself around her. Very quickly the female was pulled to the ground as the animal squeezed her very hard. In seconds, the red antelope could no longer breathe and her blood could not flow within her body. It was only moments after the squeezing began that the impala's heart stopped beating. The lady impala's body collapsed in death.

Of course, it wasn't a branch that grabbed the female antelope. It was a giant snake. The snake was a rock python. It is a kind of constrictor, which means it squeezes its victims to death.

Warden Abdi had seen this rock python several times and he knew a lot about the big snake. He had watched Rocky catch and kill on more than one occasion. Rocky is the name Abdi gave to the big snake.

"Rocky usually catches animals," Abdi said, "that are weak, sick, old, injured, foolish or careless. The lady impala was foolish and careless. She was foolish to leave the herd and it was being careless when she didn't carefully look under the bushes before she got too close to them."

After the python had grabbed the impala, Abdi did not drive up to the bushes. He waited several minutes before going to look at the big snake. Warden Abdi wanted the python to be finished swallowing the red antelope before he let Bobby see Rocky.

Abdi said, "Bobby, watching Rocky swallow the female impala could be a very ugly thing to see. The giant snake swallows its food head first and all in one piece. A lady impala weighs about 110 pounds so it really stretches Rocky's mouth all out of shape to swallow something that large. Yes, it can be ugly."

"Holy cow," Stubby said, "what a mouthful and what a stomachful that must be even for a big python."

Warden Abdi pulled his rifle out of its case, then he opened the door. He looked in every direction before he stepped to the ground.

Abdi said, "Wait until I check things out. Be ready to come when I give you the signal. Try to follow close to my footsteps. I can only take you out of the Rover for a few minutes, but I want you to see Rocky."

In the Nairobi National Reserve, Abdi is boss, so his friends did as he told them. It only took a few seconds after the Warden's signal for his three friends to get lined up behind him.

As they walked around the clump of bushes, Warden

Abdi led the way. Stubby, Bobby, and Doc followed closely behind him.

The African did not move fast and as he walked his eyes carefully watched the deep grass that grew under and around the bushes. At all times, he held his gun in the ready position as he cautiously moved forward.

Suddenly, Abdi stopped. It was so quick that Stubby, who was only a step behind, ran into him.

The little man started to say, "I'm sorry..." then he saw Rocky. For a moment, he couldn't say anything. When he jumped back, little Bobby almost got knocked down.

Rocky lay in the grass. The snake's head was only one big step from Abdi. Its whole body was well hidden by the grass and bushes.

Stubby could finally speak. He whispered, "Why doesn't he grab one of us? I'm so little that I'd be a lot easier to swallow than a female impala."

Doc chuckled softly. "You ask," he said, "why doesn't he grab one of us? Well, in my case I think I'm too big. Please notice, I did not say too fat. But what you said is true. Rocky could easily swallow you or Bobby, but not now."

Abdi grinned. "Doc's right," he said, "Rocky could not swallow you now. A female impala weighs more than 100 pounds. An antelope that big really fills the snake's stomach. It will be several days before Rocky gets hungry again. Right now I'd bet he is so full that he would have trouble swallowing a mouse."

Rocky slithered slowly around the clumb of bushes. The snake was about ready to go home. When he moved, Bobby saw the big lump in Rocky's stomach.

"Is that lump where the lady impala fits?" Bobby asked, pointing to a big bump about halfway between Rocky's head and tail.

Warden Abdi simply nodded his head.

The rock python's head was only a few feet from
Stubby and Bobby. The big snake was looking right at
the two little people.

Stubby spread his hands. He said, "His head is about
this wide. It must be more than a foot across. But even
that big a head would not give the snake a mouth big
enough to swallow an impala if it had hinges like ours.
Snakes can unhinge their mouth so it can be opened
very wide. It's another part of God's plan."

Bobby shook his head. "Boy," he said, "I still can't
believe it. It doesn't seem possible that the red antelope
is inside the python."

When the snake straightened its twisted body, Stubby
tried to measure how long the snake really was by
taking steps and counting them. It was about fifteen
steps from the python's head to his tail. Stubby's steps
are not very long, and, by step measurement, Rocky was
at least twenty feet long.

"You know," Abdi said, "I have heard stories about
pythons swallowing people, but when I checked them
out I did not find even one story to be true. In my
opinion, if a python were to swallow a person, it would
be very rare."

Stubby said, "Rocky and those other pythons
probably have never seen a midget. I'm not going to
take any chances with that big snake. I don't want to be
the first true story you have heard about a snake
swallowing a little person. I'm sure glad that Rocky
didn't have to choose between me and the lady impala.
He might have picked me for his breakfast."

The python began to wiggle and squirm through the
grass. Rocky was on his way home. The big reptile lived
in a deep pool of water which was filled by a small
stream.

As Rocky slithered through the grass, he kept sticking
his tongue out.

Bobby asked, "Why does he stick his tongue out? I don't like him either, but I don't stick my tongue out at him."

"Snakes," Doc said, "use their tongue to smell things. Rocky's tongue can smell things just like a very good nose."

While the gray-haired man was explaining, Rocky lifted his head a little higher. He smelled the breeze with his tongue. The python smelled something and it scared him.

The python tried to go faster. But it was hard to speed up with an impala in his stomach.

"Quick," Abdi said, "get in the Rover. There is trouble coming." He pointed his finger.

A large group of baboons was coming across the grasslands. It was time for a drink of water, so they were on their way to the stream. In this troop of baboons there were at least fifty members, but Doc said that some troops have more than one hundred in them.

"They are coming for a drink," Doc said, "but if they catch Rocky out of his pool, they will tear him to shreds. Unless he gets back to that stream, we will see him in little pieces. Maybe we should help him."

"No," Abdi said, "Rocky has killed several young baboons in his lifetime. Usually, he catches a half-grown youngster when it strays near his pool. We will not help him. Maybe Rocky's time has come to die."

A large male baboon who was out in front stopped. He stood up on his back legs and stretched as high as he could. The baboon was looking toward the stream. He was looking for lions and leopards, but he saw Rocky.

The troop leader screamed and jumped up and down. He was very angry. He screamed for the troop's fighters to come with him.

From the troop at least twenty of the older members

came loping toward him. They were all fighting mad as they ran and bounced in their funny four-legged way. All the fighting members of the troop were going after Rocky.

When Rocky heard all the noise, he wiggled a wee bit faster, but he was already going at nearly his top speed. A crooked cloud of dust was in the air above the snake. The python made the strange little cloud as he slithered across the dry and dusty grasslands.

The baboons also made a dust cloud as they loped down a hillside and along a narrow valley. Although they were moving a lot faster than Rocky, the python was nearly home.

Stubby said, "I'll bet Rocky wishes that he had not eaten such a big impala. The lump in his stomach has really slowed him down. That red antelope just might be his last kill."

Twenty angry baboons were right behind Rocky. Their long teeth could be seen as they were ready to bite the python.

A moment later, Rocky's head entered the water, but the big baboon troop leader jumped on the python's tail. His teeth bit deeply into the snake and cut a long gash in its tail, but Rocky wiggled his tail very hard and got away from the baboon. Then he went beneath the water and swam to his home in the pool. Although he had a badly cut tail, Rocky would live to kill again.

"Maybe next time that rock python won't be such a pig," Abdi said. "I mean maybe he won't eat so much."

"I don't like snakes," Bobby said, "but I know most of them are helpful. If they help us, they must be a part of God's plan. The plan is good, so I guess I'll have to change and learn to like wiggly things."

Sometimes baboons are very friendly. But they can also be very ugly. It is best not to trust them.

Chapter Three

Rocky the python was back in his home in the pool in the stream's bottom. In the water, the big snake could swim around with no difficulty. Water always tries to make things float, so it helped lift the snake's heavy stomach. With a female impala in his belly, Rocky would not have to eat for several days.

The baboons by the pool no longer screamed and snarled. They were now quiet and mostly peaceful. Several of them drank water from the stream near the pool where Rocky lived. Mother baboons, even while they are bending over drinking, carry their babies on their backs.

At times, a young male baboon would try to steal a lady baboon who belonged to an older male. Then the quiet would be shattered as the older male screamed and chased the young male.

Bobby sat watching and listening to the baboon troop. He said, "At times, they do not seem to like each other at all. But in the fight with Rocky, they sure joined together and stuck together. One minute they are angry and a minute later all seems to be peaceful. I can't understand them."

"Sometimes," Doc said, "baboons are very friendly. But they can also be very ugly. It is best not to trust them. They can bite and tear flesh with their long and sharp teeth. Even lions rarely will try to fight a baboon troop, but leopards do sneak in and kill them. If a leopard makes a kill, it usually carries the young baboon up a tree to escape the adults."

After the four men had watched the baboons for several minutes, Abdi started the Rover. He said, "It is time to go on with our search. I'd sure like to find the cheetahs."

The Warden drove out of the valley and up a hillside. He kept the Rover rolling along the high ridges. Four pairs of eyes searched the hillsides and the valleys as the men looked for the spotted cats.

Patience and her family, had been gone for several weeks. It is true, the lady cheetah had disappeared more than once, but she had never before stayed hidden for such a long time.

The slender African warden was worried. He was afraid that more poachers had killed the cheetahs. Almost every day, Abdi and his rangers were having trouble with the poachers as the illegal hunters tried to kill the animals. He sure hoped the bad hunters had not killed the spotted lady and her cubs.

As they rolled along a pathway with their eyes searching in every direction, an ostrich stuck its head above the grass. The big bird took a quick look at the Rover, then it ducked out of sight.

"Abdi," Stubby said, "I think an ostrich is hiding over there. I can't see it now, but could we take a look? I thought it was by that thorn bush."

The African made a sharp turn to his left and headed the Rover toward the thorn bush. Abdi did not want to scare the ostrich so he drove slowly.

"There it is," Bobby whispered, "right beside that bush." The little boy tried to keep from making noise. He did not want to scare the bird either.

Close to a thorn bush, a male ostrich sat on a nest. His dark feathers shone in the sunlight. The big bird was sitting on a nest full of eggs. There were so many eggs that there was no way one ostrich could keep them covered.

As usual, Abdi wanted to check out the area, so he headed the Rover in a big circle. Not very far from the nest, a flock of nearly grown ostriches stood up. They spread their wings and ruffled their feathers while acting as if they were ready to fight.

"When an ostrich is angry," Abdi said, "it can kick very hard. If it has to fight, it can be dangerous. A mother ostrich will defend her chicks against many small animals."

As the Rover moved closer to the flock of young adult birds, Abdi tooted its horn and blinked its lights at the big birds. This time there was no good reason to fight so the ostrich flock ran away.

When the flock began to run across the grasslands, the male ostrich, who was sitting on the nest, jumped up from the nest and ran after it.

Stubby laughed. "Look at those birds run," he said. "The way they are zigging and zagging makes them look as if they had something bad to drink. What a crazy way to run."

"Many Africans," Abdi said, "call ostriches by the name of crazy-legs, because of the funny way the birds run. I think it is a good name for them."

Bobby looked at the eggs. "Wow!" he said, "those are really big eggs. One of them could make an egg sandwich for all four of us."

"You are right," Doc said. "One egg would make several sandwiches. Believe it or not, one egg weighs about three pounds. There are thirty-nine eggs in that nest. That means those eggs added together weigh about 117 pounds. Actually, several hen ostriches laid the eggs, but only one pair of birds will take care of them. The male bird, with his black color, sits on the eggs at night while the female with her grayish-brown colors sits on them during the daytime. Their colors help protect them. Of course, it is the work of a good Planner."

Once again, Abdi began to drive in circles around the nest. Each time a circle was finished, the next circle was made bigger. After circling three times, the Rover was about 100 meters from the nest.

Stubby pointed to his right. "Look over there," he said. "Isn't that a whole bunch of feathers? It looks as if an ostrich has been killed."

The gray-brown feathers were scattered over the ground. The piles of scattered feathers told a story. A female ostrich had been killed.

Warden Abdi opened the Rover's door. He pulled his rifle from its case, then he stepped out. Before he moved away from the Land Rover, the African's eyes carefully checked each clump of bushes and bunch of tall grass. After checking, he walked to the piled up feathers and looked at them. It wasn't more than a few minutes before Abdi was back in the Rover.

"I think," Abdi said, "Mrs. Crazy Legs was away from the nest getting something to eat. While searching for food, she spotted a lion walking toward the nest. She tried to make the simba chase her, but another lion was hiding in the long grass. The second lion surprised Mrs. Crazy Legs and killed her. She didn't even have a chance to fight."

"If that was Mrs. Crazy Legs, and I'm sure it was, I don't think Mr. Crazy Legs will ever return to the nest," Doc said. "With the lady bird dead, the eggs will be wasted."

"No," Abdi said, "they will not be wasted, although they will never hatch. There will be no chicks, but we will sell the eggs to tourists and use the money to help protect the animals. Some eggs may be used to make necklaces. An ostrich egg has a thick shell. It can be cut

Many Africans call ostriches
by the name of crazy-legs.

into small round pieces. Tourists pay good prices for ostrich-egg necklaces."

Not far from the nest, a mother ostrich strolled across the grasslands. This ostrich hen had several chicks scooting around eating grasses, seeds, and bugs.

"Those chicks," Bobby said, "look like two-legged porcupines. Are those feathers prickly? They look like needles."

No one answered Bobby, because Doc had spotted a silver-backed jackal sneaking through the tall grass. The jackal was after one of the baby ostriches. It crawled closer and closer to the young bird.

Every time Mrs. Crazy Legs put her head down to eat, the silver-backed jackal crept a little closer. With her head down, the big bird could not see the fox-like animal. As the seconds ticked past, the young chick moved toward the silver-backed jackal.

Mrs. Crazy Legs lifted her head. She stood looking at her chicks. The jackal lay flat on the ground. He did not move. Even his ears did not wiggle as he waited for the ostrich hen to start eating again.

Mother ostrich started to lower her head again. The jackal lifted his ears. He moved a little bit too quickly and Mrs. Crazy Legs saw the movement. The hen ostrich whirled around and puffed her feathers, then she charged the jackal.

Now the jackal was running for his life as he dodged and ducked to get away from the stomping feet of the mother ostrich. If she were to strike him just once, her pounding foot could break his back.

A young chick made a peeping sound and the lady ostrich turned and trotted back to her family.

"Two close calls," Stubby said, "in not much more than two minutes. Sometimes, things really happen fast. First, the baby ostrich comes close to death, then the jackal almost gets stomped by the mother ostrich. Life

The jackal was after one of the baby ostriches.

The furry animals were called rock hyrax.

in the wild country is always dangerous."

It was getting late, so the four friends headed toward Abdi's house. On the way back, they stopped for a good look at a young adult female bushbuck. She was beautiful.

Further along the road home, Abdi stopped by a big pile of rocks.

There were some small animals that looked a lot like rabbits without long ears, sitting on the rocks. The furry animals were called rock hyrax. Rock hyrax are playful and they always seem to be smiling.

When bedtime came, Bobby knelt to pray. There were many things the boy midget did not understand, but he was sure God was Creator of everything. He put his hand on his chest. He could feel his heart beating. The beat of his heart was like a drum playing. It seemed to say..."I am here...I am here...I am here." Lord Jesus was in Bobby's heart. The tiny boy fell asleep.

Chapter Four

The Land Rover was already bouncing across the grasslands when the first rays of the early morning sun colored the sky. The Rover was heading deep into the bush country. In this part of the reserve, there were no roads to follow. Thorn bushes, with their strong and pointed needles, could be seen on all sides.

Dark balls, about the size of golf balls, hung from the thorn bush branches.

"Abdi," Stubby asked, "will you please stop for a minute? I would like to give Bobby a good look at one of those balls."

The Warden stopped the Rover alongside a thorn bush. When Bobby took a close look at one of the balls, he saw ants running in and out of holes in it. The dark balls were ant houses

Stubby said, "It is amazing. A tiny little insect such as an ant,is a builder of wonderful homes. How can a little bug learn such unbelievable building skills?"

Tiny Bobby reached out the window. He touched one of the dark balls. A moment later, he said, "Ouch! Gee, those tiny ants can sure bite hard."

Bobby thought an ant had bitten his finger, but Stubby was not sure. He guessed a thorn had stuck his son's finger.

Warden Abdi tried to be careful whenever he had to drive close to a thorn bush. The thorns can even poke holes in tires. Tires are especially hard to change when you are traveling in the wild country.

After stopping to see the ant houses, the Rover climbed to the top of a hill. All four riders searched the grasslands with binoculars, but no cheetahs were to be seen.

Deeper and deeper into the wild bush country the four men traveled as they searched for the cheetahs.

As they bounced along, Doc sat quietly. He looked out the Rover's side windows. Suddenly, as if touched by an electric spark, he sat up straight. "Stop!" he said. I think there is something under those bushes up front and to the left."

Warden Abdi shifted the Rover into low gear. He drove toward a large clump of bushes. These were not thorn covered. They were the kind the bushes many animals like to use for shade.

As the Land Rover moved forward slowly, Stubby pointed to a herd of zebras that was grazing on a hillside. Although the striped horses were not very far from the bushes, the zebras did not seem to be afraid.

Abdi looked at Doc and smiled, "Rafiki," he said, "are you sure there is something under those bushes? That zebra leader is not very far away, but he hasn't seen anything. At least, he doesn't seem to be worried."

A moment later, Abdi stopped the Rover. He wet his finger and held it out the window. The African was checking to find the direction of the wind.

"The breeze is blowing from the zebras toward the bushes," Abdi said. "If there is something under those bushes, it could smell the striped horses, but they couldn't smell it."

The zebra herd leader lifted his head high. His eyes, ears and nose pointed toward the clump of bushes. The zebra leader did not move.

Bobby whispered, "He looks like a statue. Gee, he is handsome."

"If there is a lion hiding under those bushes, the leader is keeping his herd far enough away, " Doc said, "so they are perfectly safe. Of course, if it were a cheetah, that striped horse wouldn't even be afraid. He can easily lick a cheetah in a fight."

The leader still stood like a statue as he stared at the bushes.

Seconds later, a piercing scream shattered the quiet of the grasslands. In a flash, the zebra leader whirled around and raced away from the bushes. He screamed again as he ran.

Instantly, the whole herd spun around and galloped at top speed along the hillside. A cloud of dust was kicked up by the flying hooves of the striped horses. They were running fast because they wanted to stay alive.

Nine animals darted from under the bushes. They ran with long strides as they loped after the herd.

Stubby had never seen this kind of animal, except in pictures, but he knew they were "wild dogs". The East African wild dog is feared by all grazing animals.

The wild dog pack chased after the zebra herd and the Rover followed along behind. Abdi did not go close enough to disturb the hunting dogs.

As the herd members galloped along, an almost grown zebra looked back at the herd. While looking back, he stepped into a small hole and stumbled. Although he did not fall, the zebra hurt his ankle. He could no longer keep up with the herd.

Doc said, "Look at that yearling colt. He is limping. The dogs will soon catch him. Why was he so foolish? He should not have looked back."

"That pack of dogs," Abdi said, "will make the zebra run in a circle, if they can. They will make him run until he can't go another step. I'm not sure, but some people say that wild dogs can run non-stop for miles. Zebras

can also run a long way, but the dogs will catch that
striped colt, because he is limping."

The dog pack was getting closer to the yearling zebra.
Already the colt was stumbling more and more as he
ran. Only a few minutes passed before the colt stopped
running. The striped animal could not run any further.

The colt zebra stood shaking. A moment later, the
wild dogs jumped on the year old colt. He fell to the
ground, but even as he fell the dying zebra kicked hard
with his back feet. The zebra's feet struck one of the
dogs a very hard blow. The kick sent the wild dog
rolling. The hurt dog crawled away from the rest of the
pack.

Young stripes was dead but he had died slowly. He
made a foolish mistake that cost him his life. Mistakes
often cost lives. It even happens to people.

As the wild dogs began to eat the kill, Abdi drove so
close that he drove them away from the dead zebra.
Three cameras took pictures of the spotted dogs with
the round ears.

Bobby said, "All those dogs look the same to me.
They have the same spots, rounded ears, and the same
faces. I know they have to make kills to stay alive, but
their kills seem to be so slow. Why can't it be quick like
many of the kills made by the big cats?"

"It is strange," Doc said, "but kills made by animals
who travel in packs quite often are slow. This includes
wild dogs, wolves, hyenas and a few other animals who
hunt in packs."

"How can cheetahs live," Stubby asked, "with wild
dogs around? A pack of wild dogs could easily catch a
spotted cat."

Abdi answered, "I don't really know, but I have never
seen nor heard of a cheetah being killed by wild dogs. I
do know that cheetahs move out of an area when wild
dogs move in. Maybe spotted cats do not taste good to

Three cameras took pictures
of the spotted dogs
with the round ears.

a pack of wild dogs. One thing for sure, if a pack of dogs were to chase a cheetah, I would try to help the spotted cat. It might not be your God's plan, but I would try to stop such a kill."

Three white faces smiled at Abdi. "Rafiki," Doc said, "if you were there to help the cheetahs, God probably put you there as part of His plan."

The black African warden nodded his head. "Hmmm," he said, "maybe you are right."

Doc leaned over close to Abdi. He whispered in the black man's ear. "Let's get away from here. The pack is looking at the dog young stripes kicked. When they see he is badly hurt, they may kill him. I would not like to have Bobby see the pack kill the hurt dog. It can be very ugly to see them turn on their own kind."

The Land Rover drove away from the kill where the wild dogs were eating a zebra. Even while they were eating it was easy to see that not all of the dogs were equal. There was a constant show of who the bosses were and who was less important.

The men wondered what would happen to the hurt dog. It certainly would die, but the pack might not do the killing. They might decide to just leave it alone. It could not hunt so it could not eat. Death would be slow.

"Have wild dogs ever killed people?" Bobby asked.

No one in the group could give the answer. Doc said, "In all my years of study and travel, I have never heard about a wild dog pack even chasing a person, but they are like wolves in some ways so I do not know. If the grazing animals become fewer and fewer so they are short on food then it would be very possible because behavior would have to change just for them to stay alive. If people upset God's plan, then anything can happen."

Dusk had come to the wild country and it was time to

set up camp. It had been decided that the men would camp out for two nights. Camping would save much time in their search for the cheetahs.

When prayer time came that night, Bobby asked God to help people understand. "Why," he wondered, "can't people know that God made everything and it was good, so they shouldn't spoil it." He gave a special thanks to Jesus for dying on the cross, so even he, a tiny midget, could have eternal life. With the peace of Jesus in his heart Bobby went to sleep.

Chapter Five

Another day had begun, the four men had camped in the wild country. Although everyone else was out of bed, Bobby slept a while longer.

Bobby was now awake, but he had not gotten out of his sleeping bag. The tiny boy thought about the wild dogs' zebra kill. He wondered if the young striped horse had gone into a state of shock. He tried to figure out why he did not like wild dogs. Finally, he realized that it was because they were slow killers.

As soon as Bobby was ready, breakfast was eaten. The four men sat around a small campfire out in the wild bush country. Abdi had chosen a camping place that was wide open. There were no bushes or trees near the campsite and the grass was short. It would be easy to see any animal that might come near the camp.

While the men were quietly watching the fire, Stubby spoke. "Doc," he asked, "are you afraid of death? Are you afraid to die?"

For a few moments, Doc did not answer. He looked out across the wild country. There was a dreamy look in his eyes and a smile filled the creases on his face, then the gray-haired man looked at his three friends.

"Am I afraid to die?" he said. "I do want to live a little longer. There are so many things I would like to do...so many changes that I would like to make...so many things I want to see. However, if my Lord Jesus took me, it would bring great joy. God has been so very

After a short period,
Pa baboon went
looking for food.
He left the Mother
baboon to care for
the youngster.

good to me although I have done so many things that are wrong. He has always lifted me up and given me a new start after I have failed. God makes living a thing of beauty, but dying is even better. With His infinite mercy and love, I would be happy to enter His house. At home with God, there is no death. I do love Jesus. He is my greatest desire."

Stubby's heart seemed to sing. He looked at his tiny son, then he glanced at Abdi. There was a glow in Bobby's eyes and a sparkle in the dark eyes of the black man. It seemed to Stubby that Abdi was beginning to believe in the living God.

Once again, the Land Rover rolled across the grasslands, and after traveling several miles, it came to a dirt road. A troop of baboons was scattered about on the road. A baboon family huddled close together. Ma and Pa baboon huddled so close they almost hid their tiny baby. After a short period, Pa baboon went looking for food. He left the mother baboon to care for the youngster.

A half grown baboon climbed to the top of a road sign. "That baboon," Bobby said, "must think that he is a policeman. He even seems to be trying to read the sign."

Abdi looked back down the road. He saw a cloud of dust hanging in the air along the dirt road as a tour bus passed the Rover and stopped almost in the middle of the baboon troop.

The bus windows were quickly rolled down and cameras clicked as tourists took pictures of the dog-faced monkeys.

A tourist threw part of a banana to a big male baboon. Several baboons bounced toward the bus as they came begging for scraps of food. One dog-faced baboon sat looking up at the open windows, then with a bounce and a jump the monkey climbed through a

A half grown baboon climbed to the top of a road sign.

window. Several baboons followed their leader.

The tourists screamed and yelled loudly as they scrambled out of the bus. It did not take long for the baboons to scare every tourist out onto the road.

Abdi grabbed his rifle and jumped out of the Land Rover. Doc grabbed a heavy steel jack handle and followed him. The two men ran to the tour bus. When they looked inside the bus, a big baboon was sitting in the driver's seat. Two more baboons were sitting in the passenger seats. The baboons were eating the lunches that belonged to the tourists.

When Abdi and Doc saw the baboons, the dog-faced monkeys looked as if they were having a picnic. The two men almost laughed, then they went to work. It was Warden Abdi's job to get the baboons out of the bus. It could be dangerous to move the baboons so Abdi held his rifle ready while Doc poked a baboon with the steel jack handle. The baboon growled and snarled as it slid away from Doc, but it did not leave the bus.

Stubby watched from the Rover. He saw the trouble his friends were having with the baboons. The little man said, "Bobby, I'm going to help them. You stay here, but be careful to keep the windows and door closed enough so that those troop members can't get into the Rover."

The tiny man picked up the fire extinguisher and jumped out of the Land Rover. As fast as his short legs could go, he ran to the bus.

When Doc saw Stubby with the fire extinguisher, he said, "Hey, I think you have a good idea. Blast that baboon who is sitting in the driver's seat. He seems to be the leader. Listen to him growl."

Stubby aimed the nozzle of the fire extinguisher at the male baboon and squeezed the trigger. A blanket of foam came out of the nozzle and covered the baboon's face. The dog-faced monkey brushed the foam off, but he leaped out the window. Once again, the little man squeezed the trigger. This time the foam covered the faces of two more baboons. When they scrambled out through the windows, the other baboons followed them. The bus was now empty.

Seconds later, the tourists climbed back into the tour bus.

Warden Abdi talked to the tourists. He explained, "Baboons quite often hurt tourists. Dog-faced monkeys can be very ugly and mean. They are not like most kinds of monkeys. Baboons have long sharp teeth and they sometimes attack as a gang. This time you were lucky, but there must not be a next time because it could be very bad. Please be careful. When you see a baboon troop, be sure to keep the windows closed enough so the dog-faced monkeys cannot get into your bus."

When the tour bus was gone, Abdi chuckled. He said, "I wonder if that big baboon, who was sitting in the drivers seat, will ever be a good driver? I doubt if he even has a drivers license."

It was late afternoon, so Abdi thought about selecting a campsite. The camping place he was looking for had to be out in the open. In the wild country, it is not safe to camp where wild animals can easily hide.

As the men searched for a good camping spot, Bobby shouted. "Look!" he said. "What kind of animals are those? They look something like cows."

Abdi drove the Rover toward the animals, but the animals ran away. He said, "They are cows, but they are eland cows and over there is a big bull eland."

The cows ran to a nearby hillside, then they stopped and watched the Rover. But, at first the bull eland did not run. He stood pawing the ground and bellowing a low angry sound.

"They are cows,
but they are eland
cows and over there
is a big bull eland."

The Land Rover moved slowly toward the bull. It wasn't until Abdi tooted the horn and blinked the lights that the bull eland ran away. He did not run very far, then he turned and faced the Rover. Finally, he joined the cows on the hillside.

"Stop!" Doc shouted.

Abdi pushed hard on the brake pedal. The Land Rover skidded to a stop. It stopped so quickly that Bobby tumbled off his high seat.

Stubby helped his son get back on the seat, then the two little men looked out the window where Doc was pointing. The gray-haired man's finger was aimed at a baby eland. The newly born calf was still wet from being born. The calf was only a few minutes old, and it did not move. It didn't wiggle an ear or blink its eyes. It looked as if it were dead.

Bobby asked, "Is it dead? Did the bull step on it? It isn't even breathing."

Warden Abdi spoke, "Wait until I check things out. When I signal, you can get out and take a close look."

The African pulled his rifle from its case and stepped out. He walked all the way around the Rover as he looked across the grasslands in every direction.

"Bobby," Abdi said, "you can get out now. Take a good look at that calf. No, the calf is not dead. It is not even hurt. It is just hiding. But do not touch the calf. If you touch it, mother eland might not take care of the calf. If she returns and finds her baby covered by the man smell, the cow eland might run away."

Bobby took a closeup picture, then he walked to the Rover and climbed to his place on the high seat. A moment later, Abdi got in and closed the door.

The bull eland made a low rumbling bellow and charged toward the Rover. At first, he moved at a slow trot, then he charged faster and faster!

Doc shouted, "Here he comes! Let's get out of here!

If he runs into us I'm sure he could roll us or cripple the Rover."

The bull eland raced down the hillside as Warden Abdi pressed hard on the gas pedal. The Rover spun its wheels and turned away from the baby eland as it kicked up a cloud of dust and roared ahead. The charging eland got lost in the dust cloud and stopped.

Stubby said, "I'll bet that bull is proud. He has chased us away while his lady elands watched. He is a champion."

"I think," Warden Abdi said, "we'd better drive late and go back to my house. For some reason, I do not feel good about camping out tonight, and it will give us a better start on our trip tomorrow. Is that all right with all of you?"

Everyone agreed, and the Rover headed home. The four men ate while riding along the trails leading across the grasslands.

When they got home, it was only a few minutes before the four friends were in bed. Of course, Bobby, Stubby and Doc thanked God for everything.

Chapter Six

The alarm clock rang loudly. Stubby's hand reached out and pushed a button, shutting off the clattering sound.

The noise awakened Bobby and the tiny boy rolled over in bed. He did not want to get up. He was not ready to begin another day. After all, it was still dark.

As Stubby's eyes got used to the dim light in the room, he could see his son. Bobby was in a bed right next to his Dad's.

"Son," Stubby said, "can you hear me? Are you awake?"

Bobby whispered, "Yes Dad. I can hear you. I'm awake."

Once again, the little man spoke. He said, "It's hard for a parent to tell his son things that are important, but I want you to know I love you. Before you came, God knew I was lonely. He brought you into my life. You have given me joy and happiness. Every day I praise God for my wonderful son and thank Him for His Son."

Bobby tried to answer, but all he could say was, "Me too."

This was an exciting day. The friends were going to the Masai Amboseli Reserve, so they rushed around as they tried to get an early start. The sun had not yet peeked above the hilltops when they began their race down the highway.

In the Amboseli Reserve, the men expected to see

herds of elephants. Their first stop would be at the
reserve's ranger station. From Nairobi Reserve to the
Masai Amboseli Reserve, it is about a 3½ hour drive. It
was about 9:00 A.M. when they arrived at the reserve's
main entrance.

At the entrance, Abdi talked to the rangers for several
minutes before he drove into the reserve.

As the Rover rolled along a trail, clouds of dust were
kicked up by it's wheels. The dust filled the air behind
them and covered everything.

"This is almost as bad," Stubby said, "as the Lake
Rudolph area. Are there animals and people dying here
too?"

"Yes," Doc said, "there are animals dying, but mostly
it's the elephants. A good number of the tuskers have
starved and died of thirst. Rain is badly needed. It is
surprising that anything can live in such a place.
Nothing is green."

They had only driven a few miles into the reserve
when a small herd of elephants was spotted. The tuskers
were stomping and digging in a dry waterhole as they
tried to find a little water. The jumbos were very thirsty
so even muddy water would be good.

Not very far from the dried up waterhole, an elephant
was seen tearing a baobab tree into pieces and eating
the tree's insides.

Doc explained, "Baobab trees have soft wet wood
within their big fat trunks. If an elephant eats the wet
wood, it helps the tusker stay alive. But the trees will
soon be gone. It is a struggle for each and every tusker
as it tries to get enough food to eat and water to
drink."

Warden Abdi said, "We cannot help the elephants.
There is no money to pay for digging wells or boreholes
and there is no money to build reservoirs to store
water. It is bad to watch animals die, but it is much

worse to see people starve. Your country is helping feed some of our starving people, but we need more help."

Stubby thought,"If countries did not spend money to make war materials and machines, there would be plenty of money to dig wells, build reservoirs and water the fields. It would mean that all peoples of the world would have to learn to live the way God wants. We would have to become one family with the one God as our Father."

While Stubby was thinking about a world of peace and plenty, Doc said, "All we need to do is believe in God and accept His Son, Lord Jesus, then we will be well taken care of in every way."

During periods of dry weather not all animals suffer. There are many kinds of animals that get fat during times of starvation for others. Lions, hyenas, jackals, vultures, and even tiny ants eat the carcasses of the dead. These animals and others live with full stomachs during the bad times.

Abdi said, "I have seen lion prides eating the remains of a dead elephant. Whole herds of tuskers will die if the rains don't come, while some animals, such as lions, will get fatter and fatter."

The Land Rover's CB radio began to crackle and its light flashed. Abdi flipped a switch and listened to a ranger speak. In Swahili, the ranger said, "Warden Abdi, we need help. There are two poachers not far from your location. They are driving a Land Rover and have rifles. They have already hurt two of our rangers and crippled one Rover, but there are still two rangers following them in our Rover No. 2. If you can't help, the poachers will get away."

After listening to the ranger, Abdi shouted at the two little men and Doc. He said, "Bobby, Stubby get down on the floor and stay down. Doc, you get in the back with them. Hurry! I am going after those poachers!

They must not get away."

"Abdi," Doc said, "I am going to stay right here.
Please do not argue with me. I have already decided."

Abdi's eyes blazed with anger. Never before had he
been so very angry at the gray-haired man. With blazing
eyes, he looked at Doc.

The gray-haired man smiled at his black friend.
"Rafiki," he said, "there are two rifles and I am a good
shot. We have done many things together, now we will
fight together. Let's go after those poachers!"

The anger that had flashed in Warden Abdi's eyes
disappeared. A smile covered his black face. What Doc
had said made him feel good. His best friend was going
to stay by his side and even fight to help him.

Warden Abdi drove fast, and the Rover raced across
the grasslands. It bounced, rumbled, and roared as it
kicked up a cloud of dust while racing up a hillside.

From the top of the hillside, Abdi and Doc could see
two Rovers coming their way. The poachers were in the
closest Land Rover,while the rangers, in their Rover,
were far behind.

The ranger's Rover was having motor trouble. A
bullet from a poachers rifle had poked a hole in its
radiator and now there was steam coming out. It would
not be long before the ranger's Rover would be
finished.

As the poachers came toward Abdi, Doc, and the two
little men, one of the bad hunters aimed his rifle at the
four friends. He fired several shots from his gun.

A bullet struck Abdi's Rover and bounced off its
hood. Another bullet put a hole in the top of the
windshield.

Now Doc was firing his rifle. He aimed carefully and
timed his shots so that the bouncing of the Rover would
have the smallest effect. He did not shoot at the two
men.

A bullet from Doc's gun struck a tire making it explode. His second shot made a big hole in the radiator.

The poachers swerved and almost tipped over when their Rover's tire exploded. When water and steam came from the hole in the radiator, they stopped quickly and jumped from their Land Rover.

A poacher dropped to his knee and fired a shot at Warden Abdi. The bullet almost struck the black man.

Doc's automatic rifle returned the poacher's fire. It sounded almost like a machine gun as it spattered bullets around the poachers.

The poachers started to run away, but Abdi's Rover quickly drove alongside the two men. A few seconds later, although it was almost ready to stop, the ranger's Rover sputtered up beside Abdi.

When the rangers arrived, the two poachers dropped their guns on the ground and lifted their hands high above their heads. The poachers were finished. The rangers handcuffed them and slowly sputtered back to the station in their Rover.

A doctor came to the station from a village just outside the reserve and fixed the hurt rangers. They were not hurt badly. Stubby took pictures of the rangers. It made them feel very proud to be protectors of the animals.

Once again, the two little men climbed up and sat on the high seat in the back of Abdi's Land Rover. Abdi and Doc, as usual, sat on the front seat. Abdi reached for the starter key, but Doc put his hand on the warden's arm.

"Don't go," he said, "We have something to do. It is very important."

The gray-haried man had Bobby, Stubby, and Abdi join hands with him. He said, "Thank you God for protecting us. Thank you for not letting anyone get badly hurt."

By the time the poachers were taken care of and locked up, it was almost noon.

Bobby asked, "When, where, and what do we eat? My stomach already sounds like an angry simba."

The four friends drove to an African village just outside the Masai Amboseli Reserve. This village had shops, cafes, and even a gasoline station. It was not a native type village.

In a small African cafe, the friends had something to eat. After eating, Abdi and Doc stopped to talk with the village Chief. They wanted him to help the rangers catch poachers.

"If my rangers," Abdi said, "could collect the ivory from the tuskers when they died, instead of poachers getting it, the ivory could be sold. The money would be used to dig wells and build reservoirs not only for the wild animals but for the village's donkeys, camels, cattle, and goats. It would mean that the Chief's people would have good clean water to drink."

While Abdi and Doc talked to the Chief, the two little men walked out of the cafe. For a few minutes they looked into the shops and then started back toward the Land Rover.

As the little men hiked along the village's main street, they passed an old broken cart. Stubby stepped closer to the cart so he could get a better look at it.

Out from the cart's shadow, a snake uncoiled as it struck at Stubby. The snake's fangs sank deeply into the little man's ankle. Like a doctor's needle, the hollow teeth shot poison into him.

Abdi and Doc were just leaving the cafe when they heard Bobby's scream.

Immediately, they ran down the roadway. With every step they took, Doc said, "Jesus, Jesus, Jesus!"

When they reached their two little friends, Stubby

was sitting on the ground. The little man was tightly squeezing his ankle just above the snake's tooth marks. Bobby was crying.

Bobby said, "A big snake bit him, then it crawled down the path."

Quickly, Doc took out his pocket knife. He cut into the bite made by the snake, then he put his lips over the cut. The gray-haired man sucked hard, then he spat on the ground. Three times he sucked and spat as he tried to get the poison out of Stubby's ankle.

While Doc tried to help Stubby, Abdi ran down the path. He found the snake. With tears running down his cheeks, he killed it!

Why did Abdi cry? He cried because he was sure his little friend was going to die and the black man loved his little rafiki. Abdi knew that the snake was a big puff adder. Puff adders have a strong poison. It can even kill big people and Stubby was so small.

Very gently, Doc picked Stubby up. He placed him on the Rover's seat. Bobby stood close to Doc's side. Tears rolled down the boy midget's cheeks.

"Will he die?" Bobby asked. "Will my Dad die?"

Several villagers had come to watch. An African tribesman began a strange chant. The chant was a song of death. The black Africans all believed the little man would die.

Finally, Doc answered Bobby. He said, "I have done all I can. It probably did not help much, but I have asked the Greatest Doctor to take the case. Let's talk to Him."

Bobby and Doc kneeled in the dirt beside the Rover. The little boy and the gray-haired man prayed. Tears were in their eyes.

Doc said, "Lord Jesus, there are three of us who believe in Your wondrous love. I have done all that I can. Now, Dear Jesus, it is Your will that must be done.

You are the Great Physician. Show these people Your great love and power. Please, Jesus, make Stubby well!"

Abdi walked up behind Bobby and Doc. He, too, knelt in the dust. His head was bowed and he still cried.

Stubby began to sweat and shiver. His face became as white as snow. He could hardly breathe. Inside Stubby, a war was being fought as the little man tried to defeat the poison. The poison was trying to kill him.

After a few minutes, Stubby took a deep breath. He breathed out very slowly, then he stopped breathing!

Doc grabbed the little man. He placed his mouth against Stubby's mouth and breathed in and out.

The tiny chest of the little man moved up and down. In a moment, Stubby started to breathe again! It was only seconds later that he opened his eyes! A smile was on his face.

Stubby whispered, "For a moment, I saw Jesus. Lord Jesus told me 'Not yet'! I could come to live with Him, but not yet!"

Bobby, Doc, and Abdi danced around in a circle!

Doc shouted, "Praise God! Thank you, Jesus!" A mircle had happened!

Abdi talked excitedly with the villagers. Swahili words poured rapidly from his mouth. He pointed to the sky. The warden was telling the villagers about the God of his white friends. When he finished, he said, "Maybe he will be my God too!"

Bobby said, "Abdi, He IS your God!"

Chapter Seven

It was the day after Stubby had been bitten by the puff adder. The adder's poison had almost killed the little man, but God, through a miracle, had saved Stubby's life.

As dawn pushed back the darkness, the friends were back in Amboseli Reserve. They had not driven far along a dusty trail when another herd of elephants was seen.

Abdi drove the Rover close to the herd, but at no time did he stop the vehicle's motor. The warden watched the herd carefully. He knew wild elephants can be very dangerous. This herd was hungry and thirsty, and that made it even more dangerous.

Jumbo, the herd leader, had led his family of tuskers a long way in search of water and food.

Stubby noticed two elephants that had separated from the rest of the herd. There was something very strange about their behavior. One of the elephants could hardly walk. It staggered and stumbled even while leaning against another tusker. Slowly, the two elephants moved into a clump of trees.

"Abdi," Stubby asked, "did you see those elephants? I mean the two tuskers that just went into those trees. Will you drive closer? I'm sure something is wrong with one of them."

The African drove slowly toward the trees. As the Rover got close to the trees, the men could see the two

"Why is the standing elephant," Bobby asked, "flapping its big ears?"

tuskers standing side by side in the shade, but one tusker could hardly stand up.

When the Rover stopped, it was still several meters from the trees. As the men sat watching the two elephants, one tusker fell to the ground. For several minutes, the elephant struggled to get back on its feet, then lay very quiet for several long moments.

The standing tusker rubbed the fallen elephant with its trunk. It blew dust on its fallen friend and rubbed it with its front foot.

Abdi whispered, "Wild elephants often take another tusker as a very special friend. I think those two elephants are close buddies."

"Why is the standing elephant," Bobby asked, "flapping its big ears?"

Before the young boy had finished asking his question, Abdi stepped down hard on the gas pedal. The Land Rover's wheels dug into the sandy soil stirring up a cloud of dust as the Rover hurried away from the tusker.

When the friends had reached a safe distance, Abdi stopped the Rover.

"Flapping ears," Abdi said, "usually mean the tusker is angry. If you see an elephant's ears flap back and forth, you had better move fast. An African tusker can easily destroy a Land Rover."

Doc said, "The elephant lying on the ground is dying. I think it has been poisoned by a dart, an arrow, or by a spear. Poachers must be in the area. Why can't they be satisfied with stealing the ivory from all the dead tuskers due to starvation? Why do they have to kill more of them?"

Bobby asked, "Why do you think the elephant has been poisoned?"

Doc pointed to the fallen tusker. "Watch its feet," he said. "They have begun to twitch and jerk. Before death comes, poison quite commonly affects the animal's nerves. The kind of poison poachers sometimes use makes the dying animal jerk and convulse."

When Bobby looked at Abdi, the African was nodding his head. He agreed with Doc.

The dying elephant squealed and squealed. The sound made big tears come to Bobby's eyes.

"Can't we help?" Bobby asked.

Warden Abdi told him that nothing could be done to save the tusker's life, but that they could end his pain.

With care, Abdi pulled his rifle from its case and aimed the gun at the fallen tusker. The gun banged only once and the elephant quit its squealing and jerking. Warden Abdi had killed the poisoned tusker.

When its friend quit jerking and squealing, the standing tusker picked up some dust with its trunk. It gently blew the dust over its fallen friend. Finally, the elephant trumpeted and walked away. It returned to the herd.

"Bobby," Doc asked, "do you know that East African elephants are taller and heavier than Asian tuskers? Do you know that East African elephants are almost impossible to train to do work and tricks while an Asian elephant can be trained to do many things? Have you noticed that the African elephant's ears are much bigger than an Asian tusker's ears? Have you ever taken a ride on a long-nosed horse?"

To every question, Bobby shook his head, but some day he hoped to ride on an elephant.

After driving for several miles, the warden stopped near another elephant herd.

"Look," Bobby said, "it is a baby elephant. It's walking right behind its mother. It seems to be marching in step with her."

Suddenly, the mother jumbo spun around. Her ears flapped a warning and she trumpeted loudly. The next moment, she charged straight at the Rover.

Warden Abdi pressed hard on the gas pedal. The Land Rover's motor roared and its wheels churned as they dug a little ditch in the sandy soil.

The mother jumbo was coming full speed toward the Rover. If she were to catch the Rover, the lady tusker could easily turn it upside down. The space between the angry elephant and the Land Rover was getting smaller and smaller.

Stubby looked out the rear window, then he pushed Bobby from the seat to the floor. He thought Bobby would be safer on the floor.

The lady jumbo was only a few steps behind the Rover. Her long tusks were only inches from the Rover's back end. When the mother tusker lifted her trunk and stretched it out toward the back window, her long nose rubbed dust from the glass.

Stubby shouted, "She is getting closer. I think her tusks could reach us now. Wow, she sure is a big one."

"If we get out of this sand," Abdi said, "before she gets us, we will be able to run away from her. I'm sure there is hard ground ahead, but I am not sure we will make it."

Stubby prayed. He simply said, "Lord Jesus, please help us."

The little man barely finished saying his prayer when the Rover's wheels came out of the sand onto hard ground. The wheels seemed to grab the hard ground and the Land Rover jumped forward. When the Rover jumped forward, it tipped Stubby over backwards. Only a few seconds later, the Rover roared away from the angry lady elephant.

The little man prayed again. He said, "Thank you, Lord Jesus."

"Whoof," Abdi puffed, "that was really close to big trouble. That elephant looked as big as a tank and she really wanted to smash us. Lady Jumbo sure was angry."

Even being careful and keeping the Rover's motor running had almost ended with lots of trouble. In the wild country, being careful is not enough. You must be alert and act quickly or life can end.

Warden Abdi did not drive back to the elephant herd. He kept going further and further into the bush country.

Stubby reached forward and touched Abdi's shoulder. "Look over there," he said. "Isn't that a black rhinoceros?"

Abdi drove quite close to the rhinoceros. He said, "This rhino has become world famous. Her name is Pixie. She is the only living rhino born without any ear flaps. Pixie can hear, but she just has ear holes. Bobby, can you see her? Doesn't she look funny without ear flaps sticking out?"

"There is more than one kind of rhinoceros," Doc explained. "The biggest kind is the white rhinoceros. It is not really white in color, but it is not quite as dark as a black rhino. White rhinos are square nosed grazers which means they mostly eat grasses. Black rhinos have a more pointed nose and they are browsers. They mostly eat leaves. It seems God made them just enough different so they wouldn't have to fight one another for food. Probably the biggest difference is their behavior. White rhinos become tame like cows, but black rhinos are dangerous."

Doc showed the little men a picture. In the picture, he was sitting on the back of a white rhinoceros.

Further down the trail, two rhinos stood side by side. On their sides, tick birds were hanging. The birds were eating insects and ticks that they picked from the rhinos skin and ears.

Stubby said, "Doc, what do we call it when two organisms help each other? I mean like rhinos and tick

White rhinos are square nosed grazers which means they mostly eat grasses.

birds. Is that a kind of symbiosis?"

Doc laughed. He said, "You can call it by any name you choose, but it is part of God's plan. When I was a believer and teacher of evolution, I challenged every part of God's plan. But then I began to study, to observe, to think with an open mind. I quit believing what somebody told me and spent hours searching for truth. Yes, I was very hard to convince, but it had to happen. I became a believer because I no longer could find any truth in the claims made by evolutionists. I can list hundreds of arrows that point to a Creator, but I can find no true indicators of evolution and I must admit I really tried. In truth, I wanted to prove that evolution was right because I didn't want to be wrong. What I am saying hurts me very much. Listen carefully! It is wrong for any teacher to teach evolution to a student. Why? Because there is no scientific proof or concrete evidence to support what evolutionists say. More importantly, if I teach evolution, I destroy hope. I erase faith. I diminish and probably eliminate the beauty of Christian love. Worst of all, I cheat those I teach out of the wondrous experience of accepting Christ and the glorious expectancy of living in Heaven forever."

Stubby said, "As you know, Doc was my teacher. He taught me about evolution, but one day after I had finished school I got a letter. The letter told me that he had been wrong. It explained and corrected his teachings. He said that he hoped I would accept Christ into my heart. If I did I would be truly happy. There was so much hurt for what he had done and so much love that wanted me to become a believer that I also started to study. Now I know without question that Jesus Christ is my Lord, my Savior, my Redeemer and the Living Son of the Living God."

It was time to leave the Amboseli Reserve. At the gate leading out, the four friends stopped at the ranger station. They said goodby to the rangers and drove away from the Masai Amboseli Reserve.

Chapter Eight

On the way out of the Masai Amboseli Reserve,
Stubby sat looking at the terribly dry land. He thought
about the dying plants and animals. The little man
bowed his head and prayed. He asked God to send rain
so His plant and animal creations might continue to live.

Dust clouds hung in the air near to the ground and
storm clouds filled the sky while covering the sun, so it
was a dark day.

Warden Abdi said, "It has been cloudy like this
several times during the past months, but it has not
rained. My people have lost all hope. They believe the
rain gods are angry. If there is no rain, soon people will
die. Already many animals have died. So far it has been
mostly the elephants."

While Abdi talked, Stubby kept looking at the cloud
covered sky. The little man had a warm feeling. It
brought a smile to his face. He whispered, "Thank you,
God," then he spoke to Abdi.

Stubby said, "It will rain. My God will not fail. You
will soon know the one true God can do anything."

It was not long before lighting flashed and thunder
rumbled. Not many minutes later, raindrops spattered
against the windshield. The rain did not pound the
plants, animals and ground, but it came down gently.
Grasses, trees and all plant life soaked up the food-
carrying water. Although some animals found shelter,
many of them simply stood still while letting the rain

Standing is shallow water,
the four men saw a pair of
crested or crowned cranes.

wash away the dirt and bugs.

The Rover had not traveled very far from the Amboseli Reserve when Bobby shouted, "Abdi, stop! Please back up. I'm sure I saw an elephant. It was only a little ways from the road."

Warden Abdi backed the Land Rover. After backing for about 50-60 meters, he stopped the Rover.

Bobby was right. Standing near a bush, the four friends could see a big bull tusker. He had long white tusks and was a dark gray color. The elephant stood quietly as he faced the Land Rover. Cameras clicked as pictures were taken.

Bobby said, "A clean elephant is sure a different color. I thought African tuskers were a brownish-gray, but they really are gray."

The four friends were happy. It was raining so now the plants would grow and waterholes would be full. There would be no more plants and animals dying of thirst and lack of food. God had answered Stubby's prayer.

As the Land Rover rolled down the highway, it ran out from under the clouds and rain. Actually, there were a few clouds, but mostly the sun was shining.

In the Nairobi part of Kenya, the land was not terribly dry.There were no animals or plants dying from lack of water, but even here rain would be a blessing.

It was mid-afternoon when the four men arrived at the City of Nairobi. However, they did not stop in the city, but drove straight to the main gate of the Nairobi National Reserve. After a brief visit with his rangers, Warden Abdi followed the roadway along the edge of the reserve that led to his house.

As they bounced along the road, they came to a water reservoir. Standing in shallow water, the four men saw a pair of crested or crowned cranes.

Bobby said, "Wowie, those birds are taller than I am!

Gee, they sure are beautiful."

One bird spread its wings as if it were going to fly away. It really was beginning a dance as it tried to show off for its mate.

Not far from where the crested cranes were standing, some Cape water buffalos cooled themselves and kept the flies off by lying in the water and mud.

Stubby said, "Wow! Look at the pointed hooked horns on those big cows and bulls. I'll bet even lions try to stay away from them."

Across from the water reservoir, on a grass covered ridge, a small herd of buffalos rested. A mother buffalo, with a calf at her side, carefully watched the Land Rover. The cow buffalo started to shake her head from side to side. It was easy to see that she was getting angry. The cow took a few steps toward the Rover, then she stopped. The Rover was already being driven further away from the Cape buffalo herd. Warden Abdi was taking no chances.

The Cape buffalos of East Africa are not like the Asian buffalos. African buffalos are very difficult if not impossible to train, but Asian buffalos can be trained to pull carts, plows, and carry packs. The Asian buffalo is very friendly while the African buffalo is almost impossible to have for a friend. But African Cape buffalos are smart, strong and dangerous animals.

Warden Abdi pointed to a big bull buffalo. "That bull," he said, "is seven years old. He is the toughest bull in the herd. I don't think that he is afraid of anything. My rangers stay far away from him and for a very good reason."

"Two years ago," Abdi said, "four poachers drove a truck into the reserve and killed a young cow buffalo. Before she died, the cow buffalo bawled for help. The poachers didn't pay any attention and began to load the lady buffalo into their truck. The big bull came out from behind some bushes. Hooks caught the men while their guns were in the truck. Hooks is the name I have given to the bull. Well, two of the men managed to climb trees and get away from the buffalo, but Hooks caught the other two poachers. He tossed one of them high into the air. This poacher was lucky. He landed in the truck and the bull could not reach him for a second toss. The fourth poacher did a very foolish thing. When he tried to run away, he ran out into the open grasslands. He should have climbed a tree like two of his friends. Hooks caught him out in the open space. The bull mauled and gored the poacher until he was dead."

"My rangers," the Warden continued, "found all four men. The two poachers who had climbed trees did not dare to come down, because they could not see where Hooks was. He had actually gone back to the herd. We took the hurt poacher to the hospital and he recoverd. Of course, the tree climbers and the hurt poacher are now in prison. It was a sad case because a man died for no good reason and three others ended up in prison."

The buffalo herd members who were resting, stood up quickly. Something was wrong. The herd members with big horns formed a circle. Their heads pointed away from the circle's center. The calves and young buffalos were inside the circle formed by the older animals. The way they were standing, if anything tried to get a calf or a young buffalo, it would have to break the circle by getting past the ring of pointed horns.

"Look over there," Doc whispered. "It is a male lion. I think he is trying to figure out a way to catch a calf or a young buffalo."

The simba was walking across the grasslands towards the herd.

Hooks did not stay in the ring made by the other buffalos. He actually trotted a short distance toward the lion, then he stopped. The big bull pawed the ground with his front feet and bellowed loudly. He lowered his head to the charge position and tipped his horns from side to side. As his head moved, his pointed horns shone in the afternoon sunlight.

The lion kept walking toward the herd, but he also carefully watched Hooks.

Abdi said, "That lion would like to get a calf, like Doc said, but he will never be able to break through that circle of horns to reach one."

All of a sudden, with his head down, Hooks charged straight at the male simba. Hooks was ready and willing to fight. Now the lion had to decide if he wanted to fight the big bull.

The male lion was smart. When he saw the charging bull coming toward him, he turned around and ran back into the bushes. The big Cape buffalo returned to his herd.

"We had better get out of here," Abdi said. "Hooks is taking a long look at us. That big bull might even decide to charge the Rover."

The African shifted gears and the Land Rover moved away from the buffalo herd. When Stubby looked out the Rover's rear window, he could see the big Cape buffalo bull. The bull trotted after the Rover for a short distance, then he returned to the herd.

By the time the friends reached Abdi's house, the sky was coverd by dark clouds. During the night, it began to rain. It rained all night long. Stubby's prayers were being even more fully answered.

When bedtime came, Abdi listened to the prayers of his three American friends. Bobby, Stubby, and Doc were filled with joy when Abdi joined them as they said, "Thank you, God."

Chapter Nine

Before the sun rose, the rain clouds had mostly drifted away, but raindrops still covered the leaves of many plants. Later, when the sun rose above the horizon, its rays touched the rain droplets which sparkled and made the grasslands and bushes glisten.

Not long after sunrise, the two little men awakened, but today Stubby and Bobby did not have to hurry. Travel in the National Reserve would not be allowed for several hours, because the rain had made the trails wet and muddy. Warden Abdi had canceled all tourists travel in the reserve, at least until noon. Tour buses and cars would dig deep ruts if they traveled across the grasslands. This would destroy some of the grass, but it would also make the wild country look ugly, so until the sun had dried the trails everyone would be kept out.

It was noon in Nairobi, Kenya. This meant the sun was almost directly overhead. Under the direct rays of the sun, the trails had already become dry enough for travel on the high places.

Shortly after noon, the two little men and Doc climbed into the Jeep Wagoneer. Today, once again, the three Americans were going to try to find the spotted cats.

Before going into the reserve, they stopped at the ranger station. After reading the early morning reports by the rangers, they studied the game count maps. Each morning, when the rangers travel in the reserve, they mark on a map where the kinds of animals have been seen. The maps are used to help guide tourists so they can find the animals. Today's maps told the three men that no cheetahs had been seen by the rangers.

On this trip into the reserve, Abdi could not go along. His rangers had found snare traps set to catch the animals. On a wet trail near the traps, the rangers had found tire tracks. These tracks had the same markings as those left by a Rover the rangers had chased two days earlier.

Warden Abdi and his rangers had been following the poacher's Rover tracks for more than an hour. Already they had found six snare traps set by the bad hunters. They hoped to find all of the traps before any wild animal was caught. Snare traps are meant mostly for the big cats. They are very bad.

In the reserve, there is a post with a sign that says, "Impala Point". The Jeep was traveling along a trail that led to that sign. They had not quite reached Impala Point when Stubby spotted some big cats.

"Whoa!" he shouted, "Make a turn to the left. I see lions over that way."

A pride of lions lay sprawled out on the grass. Doc drove the Jeep very close to them.

"Doc," Bobby whispered, "aren't we awfully close? I can count the whiskers on some of those simbas and you have always said that is too close."

With no answer, Doc drove the Wagoneer a bit further away from the lion pride.

The three men watched the lions for several minutes without speaking. Each man seemed to be thinking or dreaming. The two little men were thinking about going home and how much they would miss Africa. Most of all they would miss Abdi and Doc.

Suddenly, Doc almost jumped. He said, "Why didn't I

figure it out before? I guess I'm not very smart. Stubby, unroll the map of the reserve. Bobby you hold the animal count map. Watch my finger as I point to a few places. According to the animal count map, lions were seen this morning at three locations. We are at one location. But another pride was seen in the area called Lone Tree and still another group was spotted where the gum trees grow."

The gray-haired man continued, "The spotted lady is a smart cat. With lions seen at Impala Point, Lone Tree and the gumwood trees, where could she go and be reasonably safe? Patience would want it to be a high place where there is an open space in every direction. Unless the spotted lady fools me, she will be near the gravel piles, or should I call them gravel stacks. Stacks is the name most English-speaking Africans would use. The gravel stacks are right there. Let's go take a look. Remember, I am not promising to be right. It is just what I think would be cheetah logic."

As the Jeep rolled across the reserve, Doc kept following the high ridges. The rains had made the low spots soft and muddy so he stayed away from them.

On the way to the gravel stacks, Doc drove past Lone Tree. A lioness sat with her front feet on the sign marker.

Stubby laughed, "If that lioness were a smart cat, she would be on this side. From here, she could read the sign."

It was almost two o'clock according to Stubby's wrist watch, and the Jeep had nearly reached the gravel stacks. A few minutes later, the three men could see the stacks.

As they drove the Wagoneer up to the high stacks, Stubby shouted, "Doc, they are on the stacks. I see them. Your cheetah logic was right."

The cheetahs were resting on the gravel piles. The

Pa and Ma warthog were taking a mud bath in a pool not far from the gravel stacks.

cats remembered the yellow Jeep so they were unafraid as the Wagoneer parked close to them.

"They look," Stubby said, "as if they are hungry. I'd say that they have not eaten for at least three days and probably longer. I wonder why the spotted lady hasn't made a kill?"

Four pairs of cheetah eyes looked across the grasslands. The cats with the tear-streaked faces kept turning their heads from side to side as they looked for something to kill.

Bobby whispered. "Look over there. What are they? They look like young pigs." The tiny boy pointed his finger at three baby warthogs.

The young warthogs stood side by side as they looked at the Jeep.

"Where," Stubby asked, "do you suppose, they have left their parents? Those three little pigs must have run away from home. I'll bet the father and mother would huff and puff if they knew their piglets were gone."

Four cheetahs crept down from the gravel stacks. They sneaked through the long grass, then they ran after the three little pigs.

Catching the little warthogs was not easy for the spotted cats. Just when one of the cats seemed sure he had caught a pig, the little piglet would duck away from the cheetah. One little pig ran right under the stomach of Patience and out the other side. It moved so quickly that Patience almost fell down trying to catch the piglet.

After chasing the young warthogs back and forth, the lady cheetah finally caught one. The piglet kicked, squirmed, and squealed as it tried to get away. The spotted lady had a hard time holding the young warthog.

Pa and Ma warthog were taking a mud bath in a pool not far from the gravel stacks. When they heard their baby squeal, they quickly climbed out of the mud hole and ran toward the stacks.

Stubby said, "Where did they come from? I didn't even see that mud hole. It is almost covered with grass. Wow! Do those warthogs ever look angry. They are sure ready to fight!"

A moment later, the parent warthogs saw the spotted cats. There were four cheetahs and only two adult hogs, but the warthogs charged after the big cats.

The male warthog, a big boar, chased Patience as she tried to carry the squealing young pig back to the gravel stacks. The spotted lady could not run fast with the fat little pig in her mouth, but Pa warthog could really scamper. It didn't take long for him to catch up with the lady cheetah.

As the angry boar warthog charged Patience, she had to drop the baby pig and jump high onto the stacks to get away from him.

It wasn't long before all four cheetahs had been chased back up onto the high stacks by the adult warthogs. It was only a short-time after the warthogs walked away from the gravel pile before the cheetah young adults were once again dozing. However, the lady cat kept looking across the grasslands as her eyes searched for something to kill while she watched for enemies.

When Patience dropped the little pig, Bobby asked, "Is the piglet all right? Do you think that he is badly hurt?"

Stubby answered, "The way he ran back to his mother I would think that he is not in bad shape. He certainly has a few teeth marks on his back leg. That is where Patience bit him, but little pigs are tough. He'll be okay."

Two birds sailed to a landing not far from the Jeep. Bobby whispered, "What kind of birds are they? They must be a pair, but they don't look alike."

Doc said, "They are a kind of partridge."

Doc said, "They are a kind of partridge. The pretty one, believe it or not, is the male bird. his colors would not be good to hide him if he had to sit on a nest."

"The speckled bird," Stubby explained, "is the female. Her colors make her hard to see when she is nesting. They nest on the ground. When colors protect an animal, it is called 'protective coloration.' It is part of God's plan. Think about it . Why are those birds colored differently? It makes no sense to say that it is accidental. Protective coloration is not just a matter of chance or luck. Accidental happenings have no plan or purpose."

"The cheetahs," Doc said, "probably will stay on the gravel stacks for the next hour or more. Let's drive around and see if we can't find something more exciting."

As the jeep moved along the hillside trails, it passed a hawk. The bird was sitting on a road sign post. This particular hawk is a real killer of small rodents and smaller birds. Generally, it is one of man's helpers.

Further along the trail, the Jeep passed some trees. Vervet monkeys came running toward the Wagoneer.

Doc gave the two little men a warning. "Those little rascals are cute as the dickens, but they have teeth like needles. Be careful! They can make your hand look like a pin cushion."

A black faced monkey looked at Bobby. The tiny boy tossed the monkey a ripe banana. It grabbed the banana and ran to a log where it sat down to eat.

"Some people say that monkeys are related to humans," Stubby said, "I do not believe them. I think science really tells us that monkeys were monkeys in the beginning and will always remain monkeys."

Doc grinned. "As you know, I have been a science teacher. At first, I believed everything happened by accident. Perhaps, I should use the term "mutation." It took years of study to understand that "creation" is the

A black faced monkey looked at Bobby.

answer. Just look at those monkeys. They are too cute to be my relatives."

After watching the monkeys for a few minutes, the three friends drove back to the gravel stacks. On the way back, Bobby said, "Cheetahs are the most beautiful of all the wild animals, but Silver Tip is still my favorite."

Bobby was getting very lonesome for the great bear at Mountain Haven.

Chapter Ten

When the Jeep got back to the gravel stacks, the
cheetahs were still there. The four spotted cats were all
stretched out as they rested in the warm sun. The cubs
were becoming sleepy, but, although her cubs dozed,
Patience did not sleep. The lady cheetah seemed to be
awake at all times. The golden lady,without ceasing
watched, listened, and tested the breeze for trouble.
Why did she constantly try to protect her family from
danger? There is only one good answer. It is part of the
Master's plan.

Suddenly, the spotted lady stretched her neck and
lifted her head a little higher. She stared at some bushes
and trees that were growing down in a valley. Patience
must have seen something in those bushes, and
whatever was down there really frightened the lady
cheetah.

The mother cat chirped, and the cheetah cubs
popped to their feet. They ran to the spotted lady's
side. Almost at once, the four cheetahs started to leave
the stacks.

The cats crouched low. When they crawled down
from the top of the stacks, the cheetahs were so low
that their stomachs almost rubbed on the ground. If an
animal were watching the spotted cats from down in
the bushes, it could no longer see them. The tall gravel
piles formed a wall between the valley and the
cheetahs. As soon as the four cats had crept from the

stacks, Patience led them at a fast trot across the grasslands.

"Doc," Stubby asked, "would it be a good idea for us to check those bushes? Maybe we should take a look around even if it is a little wet and slippery. There must be something really fierce down there, or Patience would not be so scared."

The gray-haired man nodded his head, then shifted the Jeep into low gear and moved down the hillside.

As the Jeep got close to the bushes, two African men jumped up and ran through the trees away from the approaching Wagoneer. They had been hiding in the valley behind a thick clump of bushes.

Stubby said, "Now we know why Patience was so scared. Those black men really frightened that spotted cat."

There was no way the Jeep could follow the two men. The trees and bushes were too thick and the rains had made the bottom land of the valley very muddy.

As the black men scrambled up the opposite side of the valley, Doc picked up his CB radio microphone. He handed it to Stubby.

Doc said, "Call Abdi. I'll bet those two men are poachers. If they are, we have to help catch them."

Stubby turned on the radio. He said, "Calling Warden Abdi. Calling Warden Abdi. Come in please. This is urgent. Come in please."

The radio crackled and Warden Abdi spoke. "This is Warden Abdi. What is the trouble, Stubby? Where are you?"

"We are near the gravel stacks," Stubby said. "We think that we have seen two poachers. They are running up a hillside headed south from the stacks. We can't get across the valley from here so we won't be able to chase them."

Warden Abdi said, "We are not far from you, and we

are on the right side of the valley to get them. Maybe
this time they'll be caught. We have been tracking them
for nearly two hours. Rangers, let's go get them." The
radio clicked off.

Doc drove the Jeep along the edge of the trees. He
had not driven very far when Stubby shouted, "Doc,
stop! I think there is a spotted cat in those bushes. It
was standing on its back legs. It looked funny, but I am
quite sure."

At once, Doc stopped, then he backed up. The Jeep
had not gone backwards very far when the tiny boy saw
the cat.

Bobby yelled excitedly, "There it is! There it is! What
is it? It is not a cheetah!"

This spotted cat was a leopard. The big cat was almost
hanging in space. One back foot barely touched the
ground as it hung in the air. The cat's eyes were
bulging. It was gasping for a breath of air. The leopard
was almost dead. She was being choked by a loop of
wire that was pulled tight around her neck.

Doc said, "That cat would already be dead, if her
front foot hadn't been caught in the loop. Her foot kept
the loop from completely stopping her breathing."

The gray-haired man grabbed his dart gun. He shot a
sleep causing drug into the leopard's back leg. Without
waiting for the drug to work, Doc hoped out of the
Jeep. Quickly, he cut the wire with a pair of pliers, then
he scrambled back into the Wagoneer.

When the wire snare was cut, the leopard slumped to
the ground. Even as she fell, a deep breath filled her
lungs. With air rushing in, the unconscious cat regained
strength and awakened. It was only seconds later that
she lifted her head. Moments afterward, the leopard
was standing wobbly on her feet. She snarled and
growled at the men in the Jeep.

Bobby whispered, "That cat has a funny way of saying

thanks. I don't think she even likes us."

The leopard started to walk toward the Jeep. Her eyes flashed with anger and her lips were curled as she snarled. The cat's long teeth could easily be seen. The sight of the teeth made Bobby shiver.

The leopard crouched low and pulled her feet under her body. The big cat was ready to leap at the Jeep. Although the Wagoneer's back windows were closed tight, Stubby was sure that such a big cat could crash right through the glass. Quickly, he pushed Bobby away from the window.

Doc put the Jeep in gear and tried to drive away from the angry cat. In the mud at the bottom of the valley, the Wagoneer moved forward for a few feet and stopped. It was stuck in the mud.

The gray-haired man grabbed his rifle and jerked it from its case. Quickly, he pointed the gun out the front window and aimed it at the leopard. Doc was ready to shoot the big cat. The cat was close enough to the Jeep so she could have jumped right into Doc's lap. If she took one more step, he would have to shoot her. Already he was taking a big chance, but each moment he was hoping the sleep drug would work.

Stubby looked straight into the leopard's eyes. He said, "Doc, don't shoot! That cat is almost asleep. Her eyes are partly closed."

While Stubby spoke the silent killer fell to the ground. The sleep drug had finally worked. Doc lowered his rifle and slipped it back into its case.

"Whoa," Bobby said, "I'm surely glad that sleep drug worked. It seemed to take a long time for that cat to take a nap."

When the leopard was sleeping soundly, Doc once again pulled his gun from its case. He opened the Jeep's door and stepped out. Carefully he looked in all directions, then he called to Bobby and Stubby.

"It seems to be safe," he said. "You can come out now."

Stubby and Doc wondered why the silent killer had come after them. Why didn't she just disappear into the bushes? They knew leopards were fierce fighters, but even the silent killers normally run away from the sight and smell of man. Why was this lady cat ready to fight? It didn't make sense for her to come after the Jeep. Something had to be wrong. Maybe it was because she had been hurt by the snare trap, but Doc doubted it. He kept his rifle ready for quick action.

The wire snare loop hung loosely around the leopard's neck, and Stubby and Doc took it off carefully. The snare had not cut her neck, but it had cut her foot. The cut was quite deep.

Doc said, "It will take time to heal, but she can easily lick it with her tongue and keep it clean. I'm sure she will not need the animal doctor's help. She is a lucky cat, but she will carry a scar on her front paw for the rest of her life."

In the bushes beside Bobby, a twig snapped. It was not a very loud sound, but the little boy jumped over and stood beside his Dad and Doc.

Bobby whispered, "When I glanced into those bushes before I jumped, I think that I saw another spotted cat. It looked like another leopard."

Stubby said, "Let's take another look."

While the two little men bent down and peeked under the bushes, Doc held his rifle ready. If an adult leopard were in the bushes, it would have to be badly hurt. The gray-haired man was sure that a slightly injured or uninjured cat would have run away.

Hidden under the bushes, laying close together, were three young leopards. Now everyone knew why the female leopard was ready to fight. Although the mother leopard had been hurt, until she fell asleep, the cat had been willing to fight to protect her young cubs.

When the cubs were gently pulled out from under the bushes, they just stretched out in the warm sunlight. One cub lapped water from a puddle. It was easy to see that the stomachs of the baby leopards were stuffed full. The three friends wondered what they had eaten.

The young leopards were not afraid of the little men. They did not growl, hiss, or seem to be angry. The men wondered what made them change. Why did they become dangerous killers when they got older?

"Son," Stubby said, "will you get our cameras? We almost forgot to take pictures."

Doc mumbled, "It usually happens that way. When something special happens, I get so excited that I forget to take pictures until it is too late."

After taking several pictures of the cubs, the men turned around to snap pictures of the mother leopard. But they forgot all about pictures and hurried back to the Jeep when the lady cat lifted her head.

When they reached the Wagoneer, Bobby and Stubby scrambled inside. They did not want to have trouble with the big cat.

Doc put the Wagoneer's front hubs in four-wheel drive and climbed into the driver's seat.

The silent killer, as leopards are sometimes called, was no longer sleepy. She growled at her cubs and they quickly crawled into the bushes.

"I can't believe my eyes," Stubby said. "Those cubs just disappeared. It is almost as if they were ghosts. In the bush, those spotted cats are really hard to see."

The mother leopard lay down and watched the Jeep. Although she did not try to hide, it was not easy to see her. A few minutes later, she stood up and walked into the bushes.

Leopards, like so many animals, have a kind of protective coloration. It makes them hard to see in the

Leopards, like so many animals, have a kind of protective coloration.

bushes which helps them to stay alive. Their color is not an accident. It is part of God's wonderful plan.

The CB radio crackled. It was Warden Abdi. He said, "We caught them. We caught the poachers. These are two of the very bad ones. They had set many snare traps. How about you? Is everything all right?"

Stubby told Warden Abdi about the mother leopard and her cubs. Abdi said, "It is lucky for that lady cat that you came by."

Stubby said, "Yes, I suppose you could call it luck. Everything is great. Have a good day. We will see you later."

Chapter Eleven

The mother leopard was alive and, once again, roaming the wild country. She had been caught in a snare trap but saved from death. The lady leopard's cubs were all right too. With their mother alive, the young leopards had someone to take care of them. If the mother leopard had been killed by the trap, her cubs would have died. At their young age, they could not have lived if they had been left in the wild country. They were much too young to care for themselves.

Bobby said, "Leopards are beautiful cats, but I like cheetahs best of all the African wild animals. Of course, cheetahs are much more gentle and they hunt in the daytime so they are less scary."

With the Jeep's wheels locked in four-wheel drive, the Wagoneer crawled out of the mud and chugged up the hillside. When it reached the gravel stacks, where the cheetahs had been, the Wagoneer circled around behind them, as the three men looked for the spotted cats.

The two little men and Doc looked for the footprints of the hunting cats in the rain soaked ground beside the rocky trail. In the soft ground beside the trail, the prints of the four big cats were easily found. The three men followed the cat tracks.

"Cheetahs," Doc said, "are very much afraid of poachers and leopards. I think Patience will travel a long way before she stops. When she saw the poachers and smelled the leopards, she left the gravel stacks in a hurry. Actually, not many cheetahs are killed by leopards, but Patience was badly scared. Keep your eyes wide open so we don't lose the trail."

The Jeep rolled along the high ridges. After it had traveled about fifteen minutes, moving slowly, Bobby excitedly said, "There they are! They're sitting on that bank."

The lady cheetah and her cubs were near the trail. Two of the young cats were looking back. They were watching to see if they had been followed.

"Those cats," Bobby said, "look as if they were waiting for a ride. Is this a bus stop for cheetahs?"

The mother cheetah's eyes searched the grasslands. On a distant hillside, she saw a herd of Grant's gazelles. The long-horned antelopes were grazing on the rain-washed grasses.

Patience chirped. Her three cubs flattened themselves against the ground. The spotted lady left her family and moved toward the gazelle herd. The mother cheetah was trying to find a way to get close enough to make a kill.

"There is no way," Doc mumbled, "for Patience to get one of those gazelles. There are no bushes, rocks, or ditches to hide her. There isn't even any tall grass. She must be very hungry, or that smart cat would never go after that herd."

"She is walking without crouching," Stubby said. "She isn't even trying to hide. The gazelles will see her for sure. Why is she doing that?"

"Patience," Doc said, "seems to know the gazelles are too far away. At this distance, the gazelles don't seem to pay any attention to her. To them, I am sure, it doesn't look as if she is hunting. Maybe she is trying to fool them, but I'm afraid those spotted cats are going to stay hungry."

Bobby and Stubby sat talking, while Doc sat quietly. Finally, the gray-haired man scratched his head. The two little men knew their friend was thinking. Neither little man said anything to him.

Doc smiled at Stubby and Bobby, then he said, "Maybe, we should try to help her. It is not quite right, but it might even the score a little bit. Many times, I have seen tourists spoil her tries for a kill. We are tourists, so if we help it might put things in better balance. I'm not sure that my idea will work. If it does work, Patience will prove herself to be a very sharp cat. Shall we try to help?"

The two little men couldn't see any way to help, but they wanted to try.

Stubby asked, "What are we going to do? Are you thinking about driving the gazelle herd over here?"

Doc smiled then he circled to get in front of the lady cheetah. Slowly, he drove the Jeep at an angle toward the gazelles. The spotted lady watched him carefully for only a few seconds, then she trotted alongside the Wagoneer.

The gray-haired man drove the Jeep so that it would cross in front of the gazelles. Driving along, the way he did, would keep the Wagoneer between the Grant's herd and Patience.

Bobby whispered, "I can't believe it. Does she really know what she is doing, or is it luck? That golden cat is actually using the Jeep to hide her. The way she does things is unbelievable. If she makes a kill, it wouldn't surprise me if she walked over to our Jeep and said thank you."

The silver-haired man was chuckling. He said, "Young man, we will never know for sure if it is luck or a kind of instinct. However, I think God has made cheetahs a little sharper than most animals."

There was no breeze, so the bachelor herd could not

smell the mother cheetah.

"Because bachelor herds are all males," Doc said, "they seem to be careless at times. I guess it's because there are no young kids to worry about. Grant's gazelles very commonly form bachelor herds. These herds are composed of males that have been driven out of the herds containing females by the herd leader."

With each turn of the Wagoneer's wheels, the lady cheetah moved a little closer to the long-horned antelopes.

After driving a few hundred meters, Doc stopped. Bobby asked, "Why are we stopping? We can get much closer."

"Young man," Doc said, "we have done enough. Patience must be made to work. If she catches an antelope, it will be a hard run for her. It would not be right for us to make it any easier. The gazelles must be given a chance."

"Oh no!" Bobby shouted. "Here comes a tour bus. It will probably mess everything up."

A tour bus roared up the hillside and drove right into the middle of the bachelor herd. The antelopes scattered in all directions as they fled to get away from the bus. The bus didn't even stop as it continued on down the trail.

"Good," Stubby said, "they didn't even see Patience. Where is she? Where has she gone?"

Doc grinned, "She is right here. The spotted lady is hiding in the Jeep's shadow. I'm glad those tourists didn't see her. She moved so close to us that our yellow Jeep must have hidden her."

A gazelle started to run past the Jeep. It was on its way back to the herd.

Patience dashed after the gazelle. She grabbed the antelope with her front feet. Her dewclaws hooked into the antelope's skin. These sharp claws on the inside of

After the long fight with the buck
Grant's gazelle, the lady cheetah was
very tired.

the cheetah's front legs cut holes in the gazelle's skin.
The big cat pulled hard. Her strength stopped the
Grant's gazelle. As soon as she had stopped the
antelope, the lady cheetah leaped forward. Now she bit
into the animal's throat, even though the gazelle was
still standing.

"This kill is a messed up job," Doc said. "If Patience
were less hungry, I'm sure she would let go."

The antelope was lifting the spotted lady up and
down. The buck gazelle struck her several hard blows
with his front hooves. The blows and the bouncing
were hurting the female cat.

"Bobby," Doc said, "you were right. The VW bus sure
did mess Patience up. I hope the spotted lady doesn't
get hurt. I have seen her make many kills, but I've
never seen one so messed up."

The lady cheetah held the antelope's throat tightly
with her teeth. Slowly, the long-horned antelope
weakened. It seemed ready to topple over as it wobbled
on its feet.

"The gazelle's eyes are white like milk," Bobby said.
"It must be in shock. Does that mean the buck antelope
is almost dead?"

Finally, the gazelle toppled onto its side. Patience
kept biting the antelope's throat for an extra couple of
minutes to make sure the gazelle was dead.

After the long fight with the buck Grant's gazelle, the
lady cheetah was very tired. Patience stood beside the
gazelle and puffed hard for a few minutes, then she
chirped a call to her cubs.

With his binoculars, Stubby took a close look at
Patience. The lady cat had several scratches, but there
were no bad cuts. The spotted lady did not need help
from the animal doctor.

When the cubs heard their mother's chirping call,
they ran swiftly across the grasslands and joined

Patience. A short time later, the four cheetahs began eating the dead gazelle.

The hungry cats didn't eat very long before the tour bus came roaring back. It drove so close to the kill that it scared the cheetahs away. The tourists laughed loudly at the frightened cats.

While the tour group laughed, Doc snapped on his CB radio. He called Warden Abdi. When the Warden answered, the gray-haired man explained what was happening.

Warden Abdi said, "Doc, I will be there in about five minutes. Do whatever you think is best. You are now working for me. I'm making you and Stubby my rangers. We are coming to help as fast as we can."

A moment later, Doc drove toward the Volkswagen bus. When the front end of the Jeep was almost touching the front end of the VW bus, he stopped.

The gray-haired man spoke calmly to the bus driver and the tourists.

Doc said, "Please back away from the kill. You are scaring the four cheetahs. Those cats are very hungry. I'm sure they have not eaten for more than three days. It will soon be dark. If the spotted cats do not eat before dark, they probably will leave the kill. A mother cheetah does not dare keep her young near a kill after dark because of lions and leopards. Cheetahs are very much afraid of the other big cats."

The driver laughed at the two little men and Doc. He said, "You can do nothing. We will stay where we are."

When Stubby looked at Doc, he could see that the gray-haired man was becoming angry.

Once again, Doc spoke, "Mr. Stevens and I are rangers. Our desire is to help the animals. If you care about animals, you will do as we ask. You must back up. Please do it now."

The driver and some of the tourists said some bad

words. They did not move the Volkswagen, not even an inch.

Doc shifted the Jeep into low gear and pulled the four-wheel drive lever. The Jeep's front hubs were still locked in position. He inched forward until the front bumper of the Jeep pushed against the front of the tour bus. Slowly but surely, the Wagoneer pushed the VW backwards. The Jeep pushed the bus for several meters.

Angry tourists and their bus driver shouted at the three friends. They shook their fists and started to get out of the bus.

Stubby said, "They are coming after us. Roll up your window, Bobby. We could be in plenty of trouble."

Quickly, the Wagoneer was shifted into reverse. It seemed to leap backwards away from the VW. The gray-haired man said, "Don't be afraid. We can always run away from them in the Jeep, but I'm going to give them a real scare."

He pulled his rifle from its case and pointed it out the window. The tourists and the bus driver backed up quickly. But Doc was not through. He aimed at the VW and shot a hole in each of its front tires. "Now," he said, "you will all walk to the front gate. It is about two miles from here."

Once again, Doc snapped on his CB radio. "Warden Abdi," he said, "Please hurry. The cheetahs are happy but we have some angry tourists and a very angry bus driver."

With the little ranger and the gray-haired ranger driving along behind them, the tourists and tour bus driver began the hike back to the entrance. Only a couple of minutes later, Abdi and his rangers arrived. They arrested the driver and the tourists and they made them walk to the gate.

The sun was getting low in the western sky, and it was necessary for the cheetahs to eat fast. As soon as their stomachs were full, Patience chirped, then she led her family away from the gazelle left-overs.

After the cheetahs had traveled at least a mile from the kill, Patience led her cubs to the top of a mound. From the mound's top, the cheetahs looked out across the grasslands. As they sat on the mound, the cats were silhouetted against the gold covered western sky.

Stubby said, "I don't believe that I have ever seen a more beautiful picture. All I can say is, 'Thank you, God'."

"Well," Bobby said, "I suppose it is time to go back to Abdi's house. What a beautiful way to end a day."

When bedtime came, the little men prayed. They asked God to care for the wild animals. A very special thanks was given for the life-giving rain.

Stubby asked, "God, there are so few of the spotted cats left on earth. Please touch the hearts of all people and give them an understanding and a love for Your wondrous creations. Lord Jesus, thank You for this day. Amen."

Chapter Twelve

The three Americans were about to end their East
African safari. The months spent in Kenya, and the brief
trips into Uganda and Tanzania, had passed quickly. It
had now reached the time for the two little midget
tourists and Doc to leave Kenya. Before this day was
finished, the three friends would climb onto a jet plane
and fly back to the United States of America.

During the long stay in Kenya, the friends had
watched the cheetahs grow up. The spotted cats were
almost full grown. While watching them grow, the two
little men had learned much about the cats. The long
visit at Warden Abdi's house had given them a chance
to learn many things about East African animals.

At times, the little men, Abdi, and Doc had faced real
danger. Facing danger had brought them closer
together. The African, two little men, and Doc had
become very special friends. Bobby, Stubby, Abdi, and
Doc would never forget their friendship.

Although this was to be their last day in Kenya, the
tiny men and Doc planned one last trip into the bush
country. Abdi and the little people were going to ride
in the Land Rover. Doc would travel alone in the Jeep.

The gray-haired man asked his friends to let him be
alone. During his last few hours in Kenya, Doc wanted
to feel the quiet stillness of the wild country. But most
important, he wanted to be alone with God and the
wild animals God had created.

As Doc stepped into the Jeep, he said, "When I think of creation, or how God made everything, I sometimes smile as I remember how I used to be a non-believer. Yes, I was an evolutionist. Now I almost cry because I feel so sorry for those people who fail to see the truth. Being a true believer in God brings so much beauty into one's life that I am sorrowful for those who fail to accept the wondrous beauty and power given us by our Lord Jesus."

Stubby understood Doc's wish to be alone. The little man had often spent hours talking to God. It was during his visits alone with Jesus that Stubby became sure that strength did not depend on muscle. Real strength comes from God. It is a gift from Him and is a measure of faith.

The sun had not yet risen when the Rover, followed by the Jeep, began to roll along the trails. The four friends were headed back to the mound where the cheetahs had slept.

A voice speaking Swahili came over Warden Abdi's CB radio. Abdi listened, then he explained to the little men. He said, "There are two male giraffes fighting. Would you like to take a quick look at them? What do you think?"

Stubby said, "Let's go. Bobby and I have never seen two twigas fight, so we had better take a look."

Abdi turned the Land Rover onto a side trail, but the Wagoneer did not follow him. Doc kept driving along the trail that led to the mound where the men had left the spotted cats the night before.

After the Rover took the side trail, it was only a short time before it reached the spot where the giraffes were fighting. The two long-necked twigas stood side by side and head to tail. They seemed to take turns swinging their heads and striking each other. It was almost as if they were saying, "I hit you and now you can hit me, so

They seemed to take turns swinging their heads and striking each other.

hit me hard." When they did hit each other, it was a swat that almost lifted the struck giraffe's back feet right off the ground.

Abdi said, "Sometimes, a giraffe swings his head so hard that he breaks his own neck. However, it is not often that a twiga dies while fighting another twiga."

The male giraffes were fighting over a lady giraffe. While Abdi was explaining to the little men, he started to chuckle.

"Would you look at that," Abdi chuckled. "Lady twiga is walking off with another male giraffe. Now she doesn't want either one of the males who have been fighting over her."

The female giraffe was walking away with another male. She strolled down a path with her new boyfriend. The boyfriend was a big twiga. He stopped by a waterhole and Stubby took his picture.

Bobby said, "I think that twiga could lick either one of the fighters. He looks bigger, older and tougher."

After watching the fight for awhile, the Rover moved away from the giraffes. Once again, it headed for the mound and the cheetahs. The two little men hoped the spotted cats would still be there, but they could not be sure. Sometimes the four cats became frightened and moved for several miles during the night. If the spotted cats were around, the three men in the Rover were sure Doc would be with them. Bobby didn't even look for the lady cheetah and her cubs. He just looked for the yellow Jeep and Doc.

In the early morning light, the three men spotted the Wagoneer. A brief time later, they saw the cheetahs. It was a beautiful sight.

"Last night," Stubby said, "the cheetahs were silhouetted in black against the western sky, but this morning they look black against the gold of the eastern sky." Stubby took another picture.

The Rover parked right alongside the Jeep. Bobby
said, "Doc, can you hear me? I have never seen a more
beautiful picture. Doesn't this prove that only God can
make such wonderful scenes?"

Doc chuckled. "Bobby," he said, "you are young, but
what you just said shows the beginning of wisdom. If
you have discovered that God's pictures are the best,
then your faith is secure. God does paint many beautiful
and wondrous pictures for us to see, but the best is yet
to come. Nothing can be as beautiful as Heaven. God
has saved the best until the last."

The Rover was only inches from the Jeep. Abdi had
parked so it would be easy to talk with his gray-haired
rafiki.

Patience and her almost-grown cubs were sitting on
the mound.

Doc said, "Bobby, why don't you come over here
with me? I'd like to give you one last memory to take
home."

Tiny Bobby slid out the Rover's window and into the
Jeep. He had no trouble even though the window
openings are not very big. As soon as he got into the
Wagoneer, he moved close to Doc.

When the gray-haired man looked at Bobby, tears
came into his eyes. He said, "Bobby, I want to teach
you to whistle. I mean like I do when I call the
cheetahs. Would you like to learn?"

The tiny boy said, "Yes, I would like it. Do you really
think that I can do it?"

Strangely, Doc rolled up all of the Jeep's windows,
then he smiled at Bobby.

"Until you get a little practice," the gray-haired man
said, "I don't want to get the cheetahs all confused or
mixed up. That is why I closed the windows. The cats
will not be able to hear us until you are ready."

For several minutes, Doc helped Bobby. After the tiny

boy had practiced, the gray-haired man signaled for him
to be quiet by placing a finger on his own lips, then he
opened the window closest to the spotted cats. Next he
had Bobby sit on his lap and lean out the window.

"Well," he said, "let's see if I am a good teacher. Go
ahead and chirp. I'll bet you an ice cream cone that you
can call those cats over to the Jeep."

Bobby chirped and nothing happened. He looked at
Doc with sadness on his face.

Doc grinned. "You have not won the bet yet," he
said. "Just a little higher pitch is all you need. You were
kind of scared so your pitch is a wee bit flat. Now try it
again."

Once again, the tiny boy chirped, and this time, all
three young cats popped to their feet. On the very next
chirp, the cheetahs came to the Jeep and jumped onto
the hood then climbed to its roof. Bobby was so happy
that he almost fell out the Jeep's window.

"Doc," Bobby said, "I have something special to ask
you. If you don't mind, I do not want to call you Doc
anymore. I have already talked to Dad and he agrees. It
is not because I don't like the name, but I am an
orphan. I now have a Dad, and if it is all right with you I
would like to call you Grandpa. I love you."

The gray-haired man had tears in his eyes. He said, "It
seems that I'm always ready to cry, but you, my little
grandson, have made me so proud and so happy."

Next, Doc had Bobby sit in the Jeep's window. The
gray-haired man sat beside him. While the new
grandfather talked to the cheetahs, he and his new
grandson petted and played with the spotted cats.

Bobby looked across the Jeep's roof at his Dad, then
he looked out across the grasslands. The young man
saw a cloud of dust made by a tour bus. It was still a
long ways from them, but he told Doc and they both
quickly scrambled back inside the Wagoneer.

Just as soon as the men disappeared into the Jeep, the cheetahs came down from its roof and walked to a shaded place, then flopped down to rest.

Not many minutes passed before the VW tour bus stopped. It parked so the cheetahs were between the bus and the Jeep. Excitedly, every person in the bus busily took pictures of the lady cheetah and her cubs.

One of the ladies in the bus looked out a side window. She was looking away from the cheetahs. Very quickly, she turned back to the bus group. In a moment, everyone in the bus was looking and pointing at something on the other side of the bus. Whatever it was it remained hidden from the cheetahs by the bus.

Bobby climbed onto the bed in the back of the Jeep. From where he now was, the tiny boy could see past the end of the tour bus. His eyes almost popped out. He almost choked when he said, "A big lion is behind the bus. It will be coming around in front of us. It is sneaking up on the cheetahs."

Instantly, Doc started the Jeep and Abdi started the Rover. The four cheetahs sat up. For a moment, they looked at the Wagoneer and Rover. Even the cats must have wondered why Doc and Abdi had awakened them. From where they were sitting, the cheetahs could not see the lion, nor could they smell him. The simba was still hidden by the bus and the breeze blew in the wrong direction.

The lion was getting very close to the spotted cats. Doc said, "Hang on tight, Bobby. I'm going after that simba."

The gray-haired man stepped on the gas pedal. With the motor roaring and its horn tooting, the Jeep churned its wheels and shot forward. It went straight toward the lion.

When the Jeep raced forward, all four cheetahs popped to their feet. In an instant, the spotted cats saw the lion. A moment later and zoom, the cats were gone like a flash. The cheetahs were safe.

The big male simba was angry and he started to charge the Jeep, but he stopped when the Rover came roaring up beside the Wagoneer. Warden Abdi had his rifle out of its case. He was ready to shoot the lion.

The big simba must have decided that a Land Rover and a Jeep were too much for him to fight, so he slowly walked away.

A woman in the VW tour bus shouted at Doc. She said, "Why didn't you keep out of it? We could have taken pictures of a lion fighting a cheetah."

Doc answered. Each word came out crisp and clear. He said, "All you thought about was getting a picture. Your presence in the reserve is a disgrace. Without your bus blocking their view, that lion could not have crept so close to those spotted cats. Don't you realize that cheetahs are almost all gone. How could you allow one to be killed? In a fight with a lion, the cheetah has no chance to win. I'm ashamed that my skin is white like yours. Beneath your skin, there seems to be a cold heart. Could you really want such a beautiful cat to be killed?"

The lady began to cry. "You are right," she said. "I am terribly sorry and very foolish. This is a day that I shall never forget. Cheetahs are part of God's creative work. I do not want them all gone. Please forgive me."

Softly, Doc said, "I understand and I am sure you are forgiven."

Warden Abdi stuck his head out the Rover's window. "Why," he said, "don't you show these people something they will never forget? Come on, Doc. Give them a show. As Warden, I give you permission."

A big grin covered Doc's face. "Rafiki," he said, "is that an order?"

Warden Abdi grinned and nodded his head.

"Ma'am," he said, "forgive me for being so tough,
but I have a deep feeling for these cats. You will see."

He nudged Bobby and made a sign with his lips.
Bobby chirped to the spotted cats. Although the
cheetahs were quite far away, the three young adults
ran to the Jeep and jumped on its hood and roof.

The tourists could not believe what they were seeing.
A lady said, "Is it really happening or am I dreaming?
Somebody please pinch me."

Doc's hand reached up to the roof. His fingers
scratched the head of a wild cheetah. The cheetah
playfully poked at Doc with its paw. Its hooked dewclaw
accidentally cut the gray-haired man's wrist.

A tourist said, "It has cut your arm. Look out! It will
surely bite you when it smells the blood."

Instead of taking his arm away, Doc crawled to his
seat in the Jeep's window. He held his bleeding arm
right under the cheetah's nose. The young adult spotted
cat smelled the blood and opened its mouth. It stuck
out its tongue and licked the blood, then it gently
rubbed its head against Doc's arm. It acted as if it were
trying to tell him that it was sorry.

"Never before," Doc said, "has a cheetah hurt me.
This was an accident. Cheetahs are very gentle animals.
They are as gentle as a big family dog, if you understand
them."

While the tourists watched, Doc put his hand in the
mouth of one of the spotted cats. He held its head in
his arms. He did not say anything, then he looked at the
lady and smiled.

Tears came into the lady's eyes. She said, "Sir, I do
see. We all want to thank you. This has been the best
part of our entire trip."

Stubby said, "You are Americans. I have written my
address on this slip of paper. Please keep in touch.
Remember, always go with God, in everything you do.

God bless you."

"Doc," Abdi said, "we must leave now. It is time to head for the airport."

The four men waved goodby to the tourists and drove away.

At the airport, the four friends clasped hands and formed a circle. Stubby Stevens, a 'ten foot tall' midget led the prayers, while Bobby, Abdi, and Doc all stood with bowed heads. The little man said, "Black or white, short or tall, Heavenly Father we know that You love us all."

Warden Abdi's heart began to sing. It opened wide and Jesus peeked out.

Stubby said, "I think Jesus has been in your heart all the time. He has been waiting for you to find Him."

The three white men, two little ones and a big one, squeezed their black friend.

Stubby Stevens said, "Go with God. Always remember the Lord Jesus is waiting to help you. The will of God shall be done, because Jesus Christ is risen...Jesus lives today."

God Bless you All.

Patience, the lady cheetah.

Other Books for Children & Youth from

Master Books • 111 S. Marshall Avenue • El Cajon, CA 92020

Dinosaurs: Those Terrible Lizards *Duane T. Gish, Ph.D.*
At last! A book for young people, from a creationist perspective on those intriguing dinosaurs. Were there really dragons? Did people live with dinosaurs? Does the Bible speak of dinosaurs? Answers in the beautifully color-illustrated 8½ x 11 book. **Cloth No. 046**

Dry Bones...and Other Fossils *Gary E. Parker, Ed.D.*
Ideal for children, as well as adults. Hunt fossils with the Parker family, as Dr. Parker explains all about fossils — in conversational dialogue with his children. Illustrated in cartoon style, this book is fun as well as educational, with a strong evangelical emphasis. 8½ x 11. **No. 047**

Children's Travel Guide & Activities Book *Jim & Darline Robinson*
A book of fascinating activities to occupy children of varying ages... whether you are actually taking the trip described, or just visiting by way of your imagination. Games, puzzles, and Scripture exercises reveal the God of creation in all the wondrous sights you can explore in Colorado, Utah, and New Mexico. Includes helpful information for the whole family, such as facilities available at various recreation spots, etc. If you plan to visit our evolution-oriented national parks, you will want to instruct your children prior to your arrival about the scientifically accurate alternative to the story they will hear about the origin of these locations...and this book is a fun way to do just that. **No. 033**

What's In An Egg? *Joan Gleason Budai*
Many living things get their start in the inside of an egg...and children will be intrigued to learn about what actually goes on in there, and grow to appreciate the variety of God's creations. Sometimes it is difficult to explain to a child, "Where did I come from?" Through pictures and plain talk, this book tells them the story from "egg" to actual birth. **No. 185**

Stubby Story Series *Dr. Lloyd Fezler*
The adventures of Stubby and his adopted son, Bobby — two midgets exploring God's great world and spreading the love of their Savior, Jesus Christ. In a collection of short chapters, (with illustrations to capture the interest) these books are ideal for young readers and short attention spans...excellent for bedtime stories.
>   **No. 1 Adventures at Mountain Haven**
>   **No. 2 African Adventures**
>   **No. 3 More African Adventures**

Covered Wagon Boy *Kermit Shelby*
Life was exciting in a wagon train...sometimes dangerous... sometimes funny...but seldom dull! A historical novel about our God-fearing ancestors. **No. 124**

GLOSSARY

ABDI: warden, an African, head of the game reserves
ADOPTED: to make your own, e.g. Stubby adopted Bobby
ADVERTISEMENT: to tell about something for sale, a public notice
AFRICAN: one who lives in Africa, commonly a black person
AIRPLANE: a flying machine
ANIMAL DOCTORS: take care of animals, a veterinarian
ANTELOPE: a cud chewing animal, e.g. impala, gazelle, eland
ASPEN: a broad-leaved tree, usually having a small trunk
BABOON: a dog-faced monkey, usually quite mean, angry
BALDY: name for white-headed eagle, American eagle
BEBE: a Swahili word, refers to girl, lady, woman
BELIEVERS: anyone who believes, to accept God and Jesus Christ
BIG BIRD: ostriches, eagles, crowned or crested cranes, etc.
BIG CATS: lions, leopards, cheetahs, mountain lions
BIG EYES: name used for owls, Great horned owl
BIGHORNS: grayish-brown wild sheep, e.g. Blackie a bighorn lamb
BINOCULARS: field glasses, used to see far away things
BLACKIE: a bighorn lamb, baby bighorn, black sheep
BLANKET: to cover or a cover, e.g. mountain blanketed with snow
BOREHOLE: a well, a dug water source, a place to get water
BOX STALL: a pen in a barn, holds horses, like a cage
BREAK TRAIL: to go first, to make a path for others to follow
BRIDLE: a bit and reins, used to steer a horse
BUCK: a male antelope, e.g. male impala, gazelle, deer, etc.
BUNNIES: young rabbits

BUSH COUNTRY: wild country, covered with bushes, e.g. thorn bushes

BUZZARD: a big bird, a scavenger, e.g. eats dead animals

BWANA: a Swahili word, refers to man or male

CAGED: to be in a pen or cage

CAMPSITE: place where campers are found, tent grounds

CHALLENGER: one who fights a leader, fights a champion

CHEETAH: a spotted cat, tear-streaked faces, fastest running

CHOPPER: a helicopter

CLAWS: like finger nails, sharp hooked toes on an animal

CLEARING: a place in a forest without trees, an empty space

COBRA: a poisonous snake, a poisonous reptile

COPTER: a helicopter, short word for helicopter

COTTONTAIL: a breed or kind of rabbit

CREATION: to create, to make from nothing, to give a beginning

CREST: top of a mountain, long feathers on a bird's head

CREVICE: a crack or split in a rocky region, hole in mountain

CROCODILE: a four-legged reptile, called a croc, mean animal

CROWNED CRANE: a big multi-colored bird, beautifully colored bird

CRUTCH: used to help a person walk, a support

CUB: a young animal, e.g. lions, leopards, cheetahs, bears, etc.

DARK MANED: having long dark hair about the head and neck

DART: name used to refer to a weasel

DART: to move quickly, a sharp point or needle, may contain drugs

DART GUN: a gun that shoots darts, used to put animals to sleep

DIRECTION: tells where one is going, points the way

DITCH: a trench, an excavation, a long hole or V-shaped hole

DOC: a gray-haired man, silver-haired man, Stubby's teacher

DOE: a female deer, female rabbit, etc.

DUCKLINGS: baby ducks

EAGLE: big bird, bald eagle, referred to as "Baldy"

EAST AFRICA: part of Africa, countries of Kenya, Tanzania, Uganda

ELECTRICIAN: fixes electric things, a person

ELEGANT LADY: a name given to a female cheetah, a name for Patience

EMERGENCY: something that must be done at once, quick care

EWE: a female sheep

EXPLODING: to blow up, usually makes a big bang

EXTINCT: to be all gone, can never get it back

FACTORY: a big building or company where things are made

FANTAIL: a name given to a fish hawk, osprey

FAWN: a baby deer

FIRE GIANT: a forest fire, a big fire

FISH HAWK: an osprey, Fantail, catches fish

FLOCK: a group of sheep, several sheep, a group of birds, etc.

FOOTHILLS: at or near the bottom of a hill or mountain

FOSTER PARENTS: parents who raise a child who is not their own at birth

FOX: a small dog-like animal, red fox, called White Tip

FUNNEL-SHAPED: the shape of a tornado cloud, like an ice-cream cone

GANGRENE: a kind of blood poison, a bad infection

GAS BOMB: contains something that hurts the eyes and nose

GATEWAY: an entrance, a way into an area or building

GAZELLE: a kind of antelope, e.g. Grant's gazelle, Thompson's

GIANT: to be very big, bigger than ordinary, very large

GIRAFFE: a long-necked animal, in Swahili a twiga

GNU: a wildebeest, common name for a wildebeest

GOLDEN LADY: a name for the cheetah called Patience

GRANT'S GAZELLE: a kind of gazelle or antelope

GRASSLANDS: a large open place covered with grass

'GREAT GRIZZLY':   a name for a bear called Silver Tip

HALTER: placed on the head of a horse, to lead a horse

HARTEBEEST: a grazing animal, an African antelope

HATCH: to come out of an egg, e.g. birth of a bird

HAVEN: a place to rest, a place that is safe, Stubby's house

HELICOPTER: called copter, chopper, whirly-bird, an airplane

HERDSMEN: persons who herd sheep, cattle, goats, etc.

HIPPOPOTAMUS: a big fat animal, called a hippo, a 'river horse'

HOBBLES: to make so an animal cannot run fast, tie front feet

HONEYCOMB: made by bees to hold honey, to be filled with holes

HOOTING: a sound produced by an owl

HORNED OWL: a big owl, an owl with feather horns
HUTCH: a rabbit house or home
HYENA: a hunting animal, like a dog, e.g. spotted hyena
IMPALA: a red antelope, has long curved horns
INTERRUPTED: to stop something, e.g. to stop someone who is talking
JABBERING: to talk fast, to talk without saying anything important
JAMBO: short form of a Swahili word for hello, common form
JACKIE, JENNIE: a father and a mother wren
JEEP: a four-wheel drive auto, also called a Wagoneer
JUMBO: an African word for an elephant, a tusker
KAPLUNK: an expression, to fall down with a thump
KENYA: an East African country, Nairobi is its capitol city
KID: a young goat
'KILL':   to kill an animal for food, to make a 'kill'
KING: refers to the big boss, the ruler of a lion family
KIT: a young fox, also called a pup
KNELT: to kneel down, to get on one's knees
LAMB: a young sheep, e.g. "Blackie" is a young lamb
LAND ROVER: British made four-wheel drive auto, called a Rover
LEDGE: a shelf of rock, a rock shelf on a mountainside
LION: a big cat, biggest living cats, called a simba
LIONESS: a female lion, a lady lion
MEADOW: a level grassland
METER: a unit of measure, a little bigger than a yard
MIDGET: a very small person, e.g. Stubby and Bobby were midgets
MIRACLE: happens without explanation, an act of God
MOUNTAIN HAVEN: name for Stubby's farm home
MOUNTAIN LION: a big cat, (160-220 lbs.), usually brown, cougar, Tawny
MUNCHED: to chew grass, to eat food
NATIVITY: the birth of Jesus, process of being born
NGONG HILLS: hills that can be seen from the National Reserve (Africa)
NIBBLED: to eat in small bits
NILE PERCH: a large form of perch found in Lake Rudolph (Turkana)

OLD STRIPES: a name given to an old zebra
ORPHAN: to have no living parents, e.g. Bobby was an orphan
ORPHANAGE: a home for orphans, home for children without parents
OSPREY: a fish hawk, catches fish, called Fantail by Stubby
OSTRICH: largest bird in the word, called 'Crazy Legs' by Abdi
OWL: a night flying bird, called Big Eyes
PATIENCE: a name given a female cheetah, golden lady, etc.
PAW: the foot of a cat or dog, strike the ground with a foot
PERCH: a kind of fish, a place where a bird rests
POACHERS: hunters who break the law, illegal killers of animals
PONIES: small horses, named Speck and Spot, called midget horses
PRELUDE: an introduction, a beginning, coming before
PRIDE: a family of lions, more than one lioness and cubs
PUP: a young dog, a young fox, etc.
PROTECT: to keep from danger
PYTHON: a snake, a reptile, kills by squeezing, called 'Rocky'
QUISHA: a Swahili word meaning finished
RAM: a male bighorn sheep, a buck sheep, etc.
RANGER: like a policeman, protects animals
RAVINE: a big ditch, a small valley
RED ANTELOPE: an impala
RED DART: a name Stubby gave to a weasel
RED FOX: a dog-like animal, white on the end of tail, White Tip
REPTILE: a snake, crocodile, alligator, lizard, etc.
RESERVE: a protected area, a place where hunting is not allowed
RIDGES: flat pathway along a mountainside or hillside, a high strip
RIVER HORSE: a hippopotamus
ROVER: a Land Rover, British auto
RUMBLE: a lound sound or noise, usually low or deep sounding
SADDLE: used on a horse's back to hold the rider
SADDLE HORN: a post on a saddle, holds a rope, strong post
SAFARI: to go on a trip or journey, an African word
SCAMPERED: to run quickly
SCRAMBLED: to move quickly, to hurry

SCANNED: to look at a place from a distance, to check a place
SCAR: short name for the lion called Scarface
SCARFACE: a big male lion, the 'king' lion, boss lion, Scar
SCAVENGER: an animal that eats dead animals, e.g. buzzards, jackals
SEARCHED: to look carefully, to try to find
SHEEP: wool covered animals, female (ewe), male (buck), lamb
SHOCK: a condition that ends to eliminate feeling, may be caused by pain, or fear, etc.
SHUFFLED: to move with a sliding motion of the feet, not lifting
SILVER-BACKED: a kind of jackal
SILVER TIP: a name given to grizzly bears, Stubby's pet grizzly
SIMBA: a Swahili word meaning lion
SKIDDED: to slide, to stop suddenly leaving tracks
SLOPE: ground that goes upward or downward, e.g. a hillside
SNARE TRAP: a wire loop used to catch an animal, often kills
SNORTING: a sound made by an excited horse or pony
SPARKLE: to shine by reflecting light
SPLINT: usually wood (metal) used to hold a broken bone in place
SPOTTED CATS: refers to cheetahs, leopards, etc., cats with spots
SPUTTER: explosive popping sounds, a fire dying from water drops
SQUEALING: a high sound, a shrill noise, a pig's sound
SQUINT: partly close the eyes, usually caused by bright light
SQUIRMING: to twist like a worm, to try to get out of something
STALLION: a male horse, zebra, etc.
STOMACH: the middle of a person
STOMPING: to step up and down hard with the feet
STRIPED HORSES: a name called zebras
STRIPES: a zebra, a name sometimes used for a skunk
STUMBLED: to almost fall when walking or running
SWAHILI: a language used (Kenya, Africa)
SWAYED: to rock back and forth, to move from side-to-side
TAWNY: a name used for a mountain lion
TEAR-STREAKED: the marking on the face of a cheetah
TEMPERATURE: how hot something is expressed in degrees
THORN BUSH: a bush having sharp spines or needles, a bush

that sticks
TIP: another name for the 'great grizzly' Silver Tip
TORNADO: a funnel-shaped cloud, a twister, a destructive storm
TOTO: a Swahili word meaning child
TRACKS: a path of footprints, e.g. footprints in the sand or mud
TRAVOIS: a wood frame used by Indians, hooked behind a horse, it is used to carry things and/or people
TRIBAL PEOPLE: the members of a tribe, tribesmen
TROTTED: to move faster than a walk, but not at a running pace
TUSKER: an elephant, an animal with tusks, a jumbo
TWIGA: a giraffe, a Swahili word meaning giraffe
TWISTER: a tornado, violent storm
VETERINARIAN: an animal doctor
WADDLED: to walk like a duck
WADED: to walk in water or mud
WARDEN ABDI: head man or boss of the African Reserves
WEASEL: a small fur covered animal, called Red Dart, Dart
WHIRLING: motion around in a small circle, a twister, a tornado
WHIRLY-BIRD: a helicopter
WHITE-HEADED BIRD: an eagle
WHITE TIP: a red fox
WIGGLING: to move like a worm or snake
WILDEBEEST: a gnu, male (bull), female (cow), young (calf)
WILD DOGS: a kind or specie of dog, African killer dogs, spotted dogs
WOOD DUCK: a kind of duck, nests in trees, called Crest
WREN: a very small kind of bird, male (Jackie), female (Jennie)
YAWNED: to open the mouth wide and act sleepy, to be tired
ZEBRA: a relative of the horse, called stripes or Old Stripes